GLADIATOR SCHOOL

BOOK 5

D1633428

BLOOD & THUNDER

DAN
SCOTT

First published in Great Britain by Scribo MMXV
Scribo, a division of Book House, an imprint of
The Salariya Book Company
25 Marlborough Place, Brighton, BN1 1UB
www.salariya.com

ISBN 978-1-910184-20-2

The right of Dan Scott to be identified as the author of this work has been asserted
in accordance with sections 77 and 78 of the Copyright, Designs
and Patents Act, 1988.

Book Design by David Salariya

Condition of Sale
This book is sold subject to the condition that it shall not, by way of trade or
otherwise, be lent, re-sold, hired out or otherwise circulated without the publisher's
prior consent in any form, binding or cover other than that in which it is published
and without a similar condition being imposed on the subsequent purchaser.

Printed and bound in India

The text for this book is set in Cochin
The display type is P22 Durer Caps

www.scribobooks.com

GLADIATOR SCHOOL

BOOK 5

BLOOD &
THUNDER

DAN
SCOTT

A division of Book House

ROME, AD 82

Forum Romanum

Forum of Caesar &
Temple of Venus Genetrix

To the Campus
Martius

Forum
Holitorium

Pons Aemilius

Tiber Island

Forum Boarium
& Portus Tiberinus

Suburra

Flavian Amphitheatre
(Colosseum)

Gladiator
School

Palatine Hill

Steps of Cacus and
Hut of Romulus

Circus Maximus

Aventine Hill

River Tiber

N
E
W
S

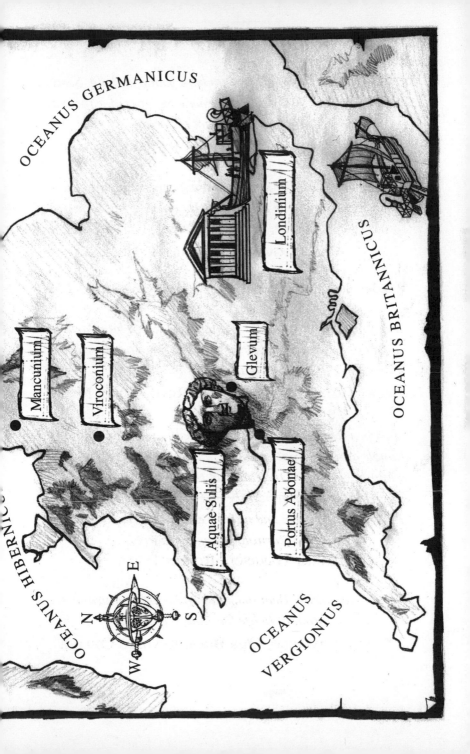

What the Lovereading4kids reader reviewers said about Gladiator School 1: *Blood Oath*

'I would not put it down.'
GRACE PARKER, AGE 10

'It's brilliant; it has a mix of different genres so it is suitable for everyone. You will love it!!!'
CHRISTOPHER TANNER, AGE 11

'It made me feel like I was actually in Ancient Rome with Lucius.'
LUCY MINTON, AGE 9

'There is only one single bad thing about this book and that is that it ends!'
ADAM GRAHAM, AGE 9

'I . . . liked the way it told you what the Roman word meant in English – it was really interesting.'
CARLA McGUIGAN, AGE 12

'If you like adventures with a touch of mystery you will love this book.'
SAM HARPER, AGE 9

'I was sitting on the edge of my seat wondering what was going to happen next.'
SHAKRIST MASUPHAN-BOODLE, AGE 10

THE MAIN CHARACTERS

Lucius, a Roman boy

Quintus, his older brother

Valeria, their young sister

Caecilia, their mother

Isidora, Lucius's friend, a freedwoman
(ex-slave) from Egypt

Glabrio, Consul of Rome

Agricola, Roman governor of Britannia

Lurco, a senior army officer

Calgacus, a Caledonian (Scottish) chieftain

Baltair, second-in-command to Calgacus

Floree, a Caledonian girl

ROME
AD 82

THE STORY SO FAR...

Until the age of thirteen, Lucius Valerius Aquila had led a happy, comfortable life as the middle child of a well-to-do Roman family. His father, Quintus Valerius Aquila, was a respected senator, and they lived in a luxurious house on Rome's fashionable Esquiline Hill.

All that changed one day in early July, AD 79. That was the day Lucius's father disappeared, just in time to avoid being arrested for treason. Aquila was accused of being the Spectre – the ruthless informer whose reports had sent many people to their deaths under the previous emperor, Vespasian. Now the new emperor, Titus, was determined to end the practice of informing. Lucius was sure his father was innocent. Yet everyone else, his family included, seemed to accept that Aquila must be the Spectre.

Overnight, Lucius and his family lost everything – their home, wealth and status – and were forced to move into a cramped flat in Suburra, one of the poorest neighbourhoods of Rome. Lucius's older brother, Quintus Valerius Felix (known to his family as Quin), decided to become a gladiator. He enrolled at a gladiator school, the Ludus Romanus, owned by their uncle, Gaius Valerius Ravilla. Lucius got himself a job at the school, where he befriended one of his co-workers, the Egyptian slave Isidora. With her help, Lucius began to uncover the mystery surrounding his father's disappearance. He discovered that Aquila had been forced into exile by his brother, Ravilla, who had always hated him. Ravilla had accused Aquila of being the Spectre, but the truth was that the Spectre was none other than Ravilla himself.

Lucius, assisted by Isidora and his sister Valeria, tracked down a letter written by the previous emperor, Vespasian, which named Ravilla as the Spectre. When the letter was shown to the emperor Titus, Aquila was immediately recalled from exile and had his property and status fully restored. Meanwhile, Ravilla, facing dishonour and death, opted to take his own life. Lucius and his family moved back to their beautiful home on the Esquiline Hill and tried to put the whole nightmare behind them. Lucius went back to his studies and Quin decided to try his hand at chariot racing. Isidora returned to her homeland, Egypt.

Just over a year later, Aquila was approached by a mystic who warned him that the emperor Titus was about to die. Aquila rushed to the emperor's villa to warn him of the prophecy, but by the time he arrived, Titus was already dying. While at the villa, Aquila and his friend Canio discovered that the emperor had been poisoned. On his return to Rome, Aquila planned to reveal the name of the murderer before the Senate. His wife Caecilia warned him not to, saying he was putting himself and his family at risk by disclosing such dangerous information. When Aquila insisted, she fled for her own safety to the home of an old friend, the consul Glabrio. The following morning, Aquila was found dead in his bed. A witness claimed to have seen a mysterious hooded figure, with a kestrel tattoo on his chest, escaping the house. Caecilia sent a message to her children, telling them to come quickly to Glabrio's house, where they would be safe. But on their way there they were captured by Praetorian guards. They managed to escape, but were later ambushed as they fled south.

Lucius evaded the soldiers by leaping into a swamp. Believing his brother dead and his sister captured, Lucius swore to avenge the crimes against his family. Shortly afterwards he was captured by a slave trader and sold to a gladiator school in Carthage, in North Africa. At the school he was trained in the arts of gladiatorial combat, fighting in the style of a Greek infantryman, or Hoplomachus. Six months after his arrival, he was drawn to fight a mysterious young

Thraex (Thracian warrior) called Tycho. After the fight, Tycho took off his helmet, and Lucius saw it was his old friend Isidora. She had joined a gladiator troupe in Egypt and earned a decent living fighting as a boy.

Isi helped Lucius escape from the gladiator school and invited him to join her troupe on a trip to Ephesus in Asia Minor. Ephesus, they learned, was the current home of Canio, the other witness to Titus's murder. He had fled there after receiving death threats. In Ephesus, Isi and Lucius tracked down Canio and he told them that Titus's murderer was none other than Consul Glabrio, the very man who had offered them all sanctuary back in Rome. Glabrio had been a friend and ally of Ravilla, and hated Titus because of his role in Ravilla's downfall.

While they were with Canio, Isi caught sight of a mysterious hooded figure lurking outside his lodging. When Canio was later found dead, and then Lucius was nearly killed by an escaped lion, they immediately suspected the hooded figure. Lucius decided to return to Rome. He wanted to rescue his mother and sister, and avenge his father's and brother's deaths by killing Glabrio. Isi agreed to go with him. En route to Rome, their ship put in at Crete, where a new passenger joined them. It turned out to be Eprius, an old friend of Lucius's from Pompeii.

Back in Rome, Lucius accompanied Eprius, who was now also a gladiator, to the Ludus Romanus, so he could sign up. On the way, they were accosted by an old street augur – a priest who claimed to be able to foretell the future. To Lucius's delight and amazement, it turned out to be his brother Quin – he hadn't been killed after all, and had adopted the disguise to evade Glabrio's assassins. Together they plotted how to avenge Aquila's death. Quin told Lucius that Glabrio was hosting a festival of games starting the following day. Glabrio liked to congratulate victorious gladiators personally, so if Lucius could sign up as a gladiator, he might be able to get close enough to kill him. Lucius agreed to give it a try. The following morning, he discovered that he had been drawn against Eprius in the fight. While they trained together, Lucius accidentally ripped Eprius's tunic, revealing a kestrel tattoo on his chest. Suddenly Lucius understood that Eprius was the assassin who had killed his father and Canio. He realised that Eprius must have told Glabrio everything, so there would now be no opportunity to kill Glabrio – but at least Lucius still had a chance to kill his father's murderer.

Even though Eprius had drugged Lucius's pre-fight drink, Lucius managed to defeat and kill him in the arena. He escaped Glabrio's agents with the help of Isi and Quin, who arrived at the last minute to carry him off in a covered wagon.

THE MESSAGE

ROME
21 APRIL AD 82

Acool breeze blew across the Palatine Hill, carrying with it the scent of smoke and burnt flesh from early-morning sacrifices at the city's temples. The security guard, Tertius Polus, sniffed the air hungrily. His shift was nearly over and he was looking forward to some breakfast. One more circuit of the grounds ought to do it, he reckoned. If he walked slowly enough, then by the time he returned to the front entrance, his replacement should be there waiting for him. He touched his sword hilt – the habitual reflex of a former legionary – and embarked on a slow, measured walk around the walls of the property.

The property he was guarding was a large domus*
near the summit of the hill. It belonged to the Consul
of Rome,** Marcus Acilius Glabrio. The Consul had
few enemies, so far as Tertius could tell. As a close
friend of the new emperor Domitian, he had become
extremely powerful in recent months, and no one but
a madman would want to make an enemy of him. Even
so, Glabrio took security very seriously and insisted
on having his property guarded every hour of the day
and night.

Tertius reached the back of the property and could
hear his stomach starting to growl. He wanted to
walk faster, but he restrained himself. Manius, his
replacement, was always late for duty. He looked
around, perhaps a little more carefully than usual –
anything to kill some time – and his gaze was caught
by a flicker of movement to his left. He turned and
stared at a cypress copse about a dozen paces away.
He was sure he'd seen one of the lower branches
move. It was probably just a bird or a squirrel. Still,
it wouldn't hurt to investigate – and it would use up a
few more minutes.

He approached the thicket of tall, slender trees and
bent down to peer through the feathery foliage. He
expected to see a sparrow or a starling fussing over
a nest. Instead, to his surprise, he saw the face of a

* *domus: town house.*

** *Consul of Rome: one of a pair of high-ranking officials appointed by the
emperor.*

bearded old man staring out at him. Before Tertius could demand to know his business, the man's hand flew out and grabbed the guard by the scruff of his cloak. He tried to resist, but the old fellow was astonishingly strong. Tertius felt himself being dragged beneath the branches along the prickly, needle-covered ground.

He tried to bellow, but a hand clamped down hard on his mouth. He twisted towards his captor and saw not just one but three old men staring down at him – all with grizzled faces and long grey beards. Tertius tried to reach for his sword, but a knee pressed fiercely against his arm, pinning it to his side. He stared wildly up at the old men, fearing he was about to be murdered. Tertius could only watch helplessly as one of them raised a club above his head and brought it down. Then everything went black.

'You shouldn't have done that,' said Lucius, scratching his chin – the fake beard was becoming very itchy.

'What else could I do?' replied Quin.

'We could have taken him prisoner,' suggested Isidora.

'And tied him up with *what*?' demanded Quin. He sighed and shook his head, causing a small shower of hair-whitening powder to cascade onto his shoulders. 'I'm working with amateurs here! You two have no idea about covert operations, do you?'

'We'd better do what we came here for,' said Lucius, pulling a heavy round stone from his canvas bag. The stone was wrapped in a sheet of papyrus,* secured by some string.

'Are you absolutely sure no one in the house will understand that note?' asked Isi.

'Of course I am,' Lucius assured her. 'It's written in a code Val and I used when we were children – it'll be gibberish to anyone but her.'

'What does it say?' asked Quin.

'It says we're still alive and it gives the location of our hideout by the river.'

'Oh, great!' grunted Quin. 'So if we wake up tomorrow and find ourselves surrounded by a cohort of Praetorian guards,** I'll know who to blame!'

'Which window is hers, do you think?' asked Isi.

Lucius contemplated the row of three small windows in the upper part of the wall. Their shutters had been opened, but the interiors were too dark to see inside. 'I'm sure Val's bedroom is the middle one,' he said after a while.

'You're wrong,' said Quin firmly. 'It's the one on the right. Val had the corner room in our old house, and she'll have chosen the corner room here, too.'

'But she never liked that room...'

'Rubbish!' said Quin. 'See how the dawn light

---

* papyrus: paper made from an Egyptian reed.

** Praetorian guards: the emperor's elite bodyguard.

catches the window there. Our dear sister always did adore the morning sun. That's definitely her room.'

In the shadows below them, the guard moaned and blinked. Quin hit him again.

'You two had better pick a window soon,' said Isi. 'This place'll be crawling with guards once they notice this one hasn't come back.'

'It's the middle window,' decided Lucius.

'No it's not!' said Quin.

'Look, it doesn't matter which window you choose,' cried Isi, puffing through her beard in exasperation. 'Just throw it into one of them so we can get out of here.'

Lucius glanced from side to side before emerging from the thicket. He began to run in quick loping strides towards the house, then stopped. Something had appeared briefly at the one window they'd neglected to consider – the one on the left. It was only there for a second, but he could swear he'd seen an arm – quite a long arm, possibly covered in dark fur…

Simio the chimpanzee – Val's constant companion!

He moved to a position below that window and took aim. Behind him, he could hear Quin's hissed 'What are you doing?' and ignored it. Leaning back, Lucius hurled the stone with note attached through the open window. It was a perfect throw, and he heard the muffled clink as it bounced on the floor tiles inside the bedroom. This was followed by a short cry of surprise. He dived back into the clump of cypresses just as a face appeared at the window. For an excited moment he thought it was his mother – but it wasn't. It was no one he recognised – a slave, to judge from her clothing.

'What were you doing throwing it in *that* window?' Quin wanted to know.

'I thought I saw Simio there.'

'Really?' They both looked at him sceptically.

'Really!' replied an indignant Lucius.

Just then, they heard running footsteps approaching from the front of the house.

'Guards!' hissed Isi.

The trio hastily retreated into the grove of cypresses that separated Glabrio's house from its neighbours. They joined a path taking them towards the southwestern spur of the Palatine Hill. Lucius wanted to run, but he knew that would only make them look suspicious. As they descended the twisting path, he kept a wary eye out for Praetorian guards. Just two days earlier, Lucius had killed his father's murderer, Eprius, in hand-to-hand combat in the arena. And now Glabrio, who had hired Eprius to kill Lucius, was scouring the city in search of him. The Praetorians seemed to be everywhere, patrolling the streets on horseback or in tight infantry formations. It was an intimidating sight for Rome's citizens, and most especially for Lucius. They'd had to clear out of Quin's shack in the Suburra district, as Eprius was sure to have told Glabrio where it was. They had moved into the cellar of an abandoned riverfront tavern near the vegetable market, the Forum Holitorium.

Their disguises had kept them reasonably safe until now. But as soon as that guard revived, he'd report what had happened to his master, and Glabrio would immediately guess the true identity of the three 'old men'. Then the whole city would be on the lookout for them. They'd have to change their appearances once again! Lucius recalled the hours of painstaking work Quin had spent on their disguise. Using a slender brush, he'd carefully applied ground-up lead sulphide to give the appearance of shadows, wrinkles, hollow cheeks and sagging skin. The effect was completed by whitening their hair with powder and donning grey beards. He wondered what Quin would turn them into now.

As they walked past the litters* of the wealthy being carried down the hill towards the Forum Romanum,** Lucius imagined curious eyes peering out at him from behind the litter curtains. He lowered his head as they passed a group of priests visiting the Hut of Romulus, the legendary dwelling of the first king of Rome. This one-room peasant hut, with straw roof and wattle-and-daub walls, stood in stark contrast to the palatial residences nearby.

'Once we've made contact with Val, we should get out of Rome,' Lucius muttered. 'It's too dangerous

* *litters: chairs or beds carried on poles.*

** *Forum Romanum: Rome's main marketplace, which was also the place for business meetings and political discussions.*

here. And I'm tired of being scared all the time.'

'You go if you like,' said Quin, 'but I'm not leaving – not until Valeria and mother are safe, and Glabrio is dead.'

'Don't you think we should lie low for a while?' argued Lucius. 'Let him think we've disappeared – then return when we're ready, when he's least expecting us, and kill him then.'

'There you two go again,' said Isi. 'You know you'll never get near the man. You saw just now how carefully he guards his house.'

Not far from the Hut of Romulus lay the Steps of Cacus. This ornamental stairway, decorated with terraced flowerbeds, wound down the side of the hill towards the crowded cattle market, or Forum Boarium, and beyond that to the river. Once they were back amongst the bustle of the meat and fish stalls, Lucius felt a little safer – here he could imagine himself almost as anonymous as a mackerel among the thousands arriving by cartload from the docks. After passing through the market, they walked along the riverfront, heading north towards their hideout near the Forum Holitorium.

'What are all those people doing down there by the riverbank?' asked Isi suddenly. The other two turned to see where she was pointing. They had just passed the multi-arched bridge known as the Pons Aemilius, where the River Tiber bent westwards along the southern border of the Campus Martius.* On the muddy banks near the first of the bridge's arches, a small group of people had gathered. A couple of them were dragging something out of the water. Lucius, Quin and Isi drew closer, and let out a collective gasp when they saw what it was: the body of a man.

* *Campus Martius: the Field of Mars, an area to the northwest of the city centre which had many fine public buildings.*

PART ONE

THE BODY IN THE RIVER

CHAPTER I

21–22 APRIL

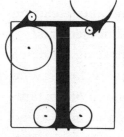he dead man's flesh was mottled and bluish after its long submersion in water. There were signs of bruising on his skin. His grey hair and the bald spot on his crown gave Lucius the impression of a meek and gentle man, undeserving of this horrid fate.

'He's probably just an old slave from Tiber Island who'd had enough,' said Quin. Tiber Island was an islet in the middle of the river just a short way upstream. It was inhabited by elderly or sick slaves who had been abandoned by their masters.

'But look at his toga,' said Isi. 'He must have been wealthy.'

The boys looked, and had to agree with her. The

toga, though sodden and caked in the filth of the river, appeared to be of good-quality material.

A cry went up from one of the women gathered near the body: 'Gods! It's Diomedes!'

The news passed swiftly among the others on the riverbank, and Lucius heard the name repeated like an echo: 'It's Diomedes!... Diomedes!... Diomedes!' Even those who had congregated on the bridge above, and on the waterfront, took up the cry. 'Diomedes... Diomedes is dead!'

'Who is Diomedes?' one young man nervously asked.

'You don't know who Diomedes is?' another accused him, before turning to his friend and declaring incredulously: 'He doesn't know who Diomedes is!'

From the general confused muttering, Lucius concluded that not many people actually knew who Diomedes was, only that he was someone important. Lucius himself thought he'd heard the name mentioned once or twice, possibly by his father, but he, too, couldn't remember who the man was. Eventually, the woman who'd originally identified him put everyone out of their misery. 'Diomedes,' she said, 'was personal physician to our beloved former emperor and now god, Titus.'

Everyone then turned with renewed interest to the corpse lying on the mud, getting splashed by the murky brown waters of the river. It seemed almost impossible to believe that those blotchy, swollen hands had once tended to the medical needs of the most powerful man on earth.

Later, as they walked homewards, Lucius tried to dredge up his memories of Diomedes. He was a great physician, without question – perhaps the greatest of his era. Lucius seemed to recall his father once mentioning that he was a humble man despite his reputation, living modestly with his wife on the Aventine Hill.

Isi then voiced the question that had been preoccupying them all: 'Why would a successful physician kill himself?'

'If he *did* kill himself,' said Lucius.

Quin frowned at him. 'Are you suggesting he was murdered? For what reason? It wasn't his fault that Titus died.'

'No, but he must have been there in the villa,' said Lucius, 'just like father and Canio. He's now the third person to have died among those who attended Titus in his final hours.'

'What are you saying, Lucius?' asked Isi.

'I don't know what I'm saying – only that I think this merits further investigation… Perhaps we should go and visit his widow. Their house is on the Aventine. She might be able to tell us something.'

'Good idea,' said Lucius.

The following morning, Lucius, Quin and Isi arrived at the house of Diomedes's widow, Claudia. After a fierce debate about what manner of identity they should adopt now that their 'old men' disguise had been blown, they decided that Quin should play the part of a young noble, new to Rome – a former patient of Diomedes who had come to pay his respects. Lucius and Isidora would be his slaves.

The house was large and built on the western slope of the hill, close to the summit. The entrance was grand in scale, with a six-pillared portico,* reflecting the late physician's status. Cypress branches had been placed above the doorway – the sign of a house in mourning.

Quin offered the porter his most disarming smile and introduced himself. 'My name,' he said, 'is Spurius Fabulus. I have lately arrived from Cremona** and heard the tragic news of your master's death. I have come to pay my respects to your mistress.'

Lucius felt a giggle forming uncontrollably in his throat. Quin looked and sounded ridiculous. He had used a mixture of honey, cider vinegar and rose petals to lighten his already golden curls to a colour closer to blond. He'd used crushed berries to darken his lips, and put black kohl on his eyes. Sometimes,

* *portico: a porch with columns.*

** *Cremona: a Roman city in the north of Italy.*

Lucius suspected Quin enjoyed this whole business of disguise just a little too much.

The porter shot Lucius a glare, and he felt himself flush under the scrutiny. He worried that the white lead foundation that Quin had applied to his face that morning would crack, and, even worse, that his nose would fall off. Quin had mixed up a paste of oil, wax and clay and used this to enlarge Lucius's nose. He'd added a fake scar to his cheek for good measure. It all felt a bit precarious, as if it might collapse if he so much as smiled.

'So don't smile,' had been Quin's advice when he'd mentioned this earlier. 'You're a slave, aren't you? What possible reason would you have to smile?'

Lucius bit his lip and dipped his head submissively, as a slave might. He envied Isi. Being unknown to Glabrio, she required the least make-up. With her cropped hair and baggy men's tunic, she easily passed for a boy.

'The mistress is indisposed,' said the porter. 'She is not seeing anyone today. I shall tell her you called. What exactly is your connection with the master?'

'I had the great honour of being cured by him,' said Spurius Fabulus. 'I had a most severe case of... of...' Quin did not appear to have thought this part of his story through in sufficient detail, probably trusting that charm would see him through. Sometimes, Lucius reckoned, his brother relied a little too much on his charm. 'A severe case of warts,' Quin said finally.

Warts? What was he thinking of?

'Warts?' frowned the porter.

'Covered in them, I was,' sighed Quin. 'From head to toe. You wouldn't believe it looking at me now, of course, but I was not a pretty sight. Then I met your master, Diomedes, and he prescribed, er... silphium,* I think it was, and they cleared up almost overnight.'

'Indeed,' said the porter, looking unimpressed. 'I'm glad to hear it. And thank you for taking the trouble to visit. I shall tell my mistress you called. Good day.'

This was not going as planned. Quin stood there, mouth flapping open and shut, as the porter waited for them to leave.

Then Isi spoke: 'It's possible your mistress has some questions about her husband's death. We may be able to help provide the answers.'

Lucius, Quin and the porter all stared at her.

'Your slave speaks for you?' queried the porter.

'My slave...' said Quin with a furious glare at Isi, 'sometimes forgets his place... But, yes, he speaks the truth. We may have some answers for your mistress.'

The porter considered this for a moment, then said: 'Wait here,' and disappeared into the house.

When they were alone, Quin turned on Isi. 'What are you playing at? What answers are we going to give her? We know nothing about why her husband died.'

'I had to say something,' said Isi defensively. 'You

* *silphium: a plant used in ancient medicine. Scholars today are not sure what it was.*

were getting us nowhere with your warts story.'

'I was… improvising,' said Quin limply. 'I'd have thought of something, given time.'

A few minutes later, the porter returned, along with the steward, a burly, stiff-shouldered type, who asked them to follow him. The steward led them through the atrium into a peristyled courtyard.* Lucius couldn't help noticing that the man had a limp in his left leg, which he tried to disguise with his erect carriage and military style of walking. He escorted them through the tablinum – the master's study, where a bust of Titus stood prominently near the desk – and out into the hortus, a garden filled with flowering shrubs. The rear wall of the garden had arched openings, offering a spectacular view to the west. It was here that they found the mistress, Claudia, seated on a stone bench next to a Grecian urn. She was perhaps fifty years old, and dressed in the white of mourning. Her grey hair hung loose around her shoulders.

She did not dismiss the steward, who remained standing stiffly to attention as Quin stepped forward to introduce himself. 'Madam, I'm most honoured,' he said with a bow.

She looked him up and down, then returned her attention to the view. 'My husband was never in Cremona,' was her only comment.

Quin began to splutter something when she interrupted. 'Tell me who you really are, and then we

* atrium: entrance courtyard; peristyled: surrounded by columns.

can talk.'

After exchanging an anxious glance with Lucius, Quin said weakly: 'I'm afraid I cannot.'

Claudia looked on the point of ejecting them, but then seemed to think better of it. She indicated the scene through the arched opening in the wall. 'You know, I've never liked this view,' she said.

Lucius wondered why she would choose to mention such a fact. He looked through the arch and observed the houses, tenements and artisan workshops clustered on the lower slopes of the Aventine Hill. Beyond that lay the granaries and warehouses lining the Tiber. The creamy-brown river gleamed in the hazy morning light as it wound its way through the city towards the woods and meadows in the west. It was a perfectly lovely vista, he thought, and he couldn't see why she would object to it.

'My husband insisted on living here,' Claudia continued. 'I would have much preferred to live on the north side of the Aventine, which is so much more fashionable. I used to say to him, "Diomedes, wouldn't you rather look out upon the Circus Maximus* and the Palatine Hill than shabby tenements and a polluted river?" We could easily have afforded a place over there – but he had a fondness for this house, and this view. The river calmed him, I think. It reminded him that there was a world beyond Rome... He was

---

* *Circus Maximus: the great stadium for chariot races. It stood to the south of the Palatine Hill, one of the oldest and most exclusive parts of the city.*

the most famous physician in the city, you know. He counted consuls and emperors among his patients. Yet however powerful he became, however rich, he remained untouched by any of it. Like the Tiber, he flowed through this city, but he came from a purer source. He would not be corrupted. That was why, in the end, he had to die.'

This last sentence made Lucius's ears prick up.

'Are you saying your husband was murdered?' asked Quin.

'Undoubtedly,' said the widow.

'Could it not have been an accident?'

She gave Quin a stern look. 'My husband may have loved the river, but he would never have gone swimming in it.' Her gaze dropped to her lap where her hands were slowly twisting the fabric of her stola.* 'I knew Diomedes had been murdered long before they found his body yesterday. I knew it when he went missing four weeks ago. He wasn't the type to run away from his troubles.'

'But who would kill him?' blurted out Lucius, forgetting he was supposed to be a slave.

Claudia regarded him closely. 'First tell me who I'm talking to.'

Lucius felt the sweat start to seep through the cracks in his make-up. For all he knew, this woman might be a friend of Glabrio's.

The widow, sensing his nervousness, said: 'You

_____
* *stola: a long dress worn by respectable married women.*

have nothing to fear from me.'

Lucius read honesty in her steady grey eyes. He wanted to trust her. His gaze flickered towards the steward who was still standing there, back ruler-straight, eyes front, face like stone. But slaves were known to listen – and talk.

Claudia read his fear. 'Do not worry about Demetrius,' she said. 'He is utterly loyal – aren't you, Demetrius?'

'Yes, my lady,' he said without a trace of emotion. Lucius guessed from his demeanour that he had a military background.

'Anything you say to me you can say to Demetrius,' Claudia reassured them. 'He's been a good friend to us for many years – since my husband's days as a battlefield surgeon, in fact. You were an optio* back then, were you not, Demetrius?'

'Yes, my lady.'

'Diomedes saved Demetrius's leg after an arrow passed straight through it,' explained Claudia. 'They became friends and, on his retirement a few years ago, Demetrius came to work for us. So, you see, you have nothing to worry about... Now, you said that you might be able to shed some light on the mystery of my husband's death. I'd like to hear what you have to say. But first I must insist on knowing who you are.' She waited for them to speak. When they didn't, she added: 'I can see that you've disguised yourselves.

* *optio: a centurion's second-in-command.*

Your make-up is rather... garish – you look like a chorus* from the theatre. I assume you're hiding from someone. If it's the authorities, then fear not. I am no friend of the people currently in charge.'

Lucius glanced at his companions. Isi didn't meet his eyes, but Quin did, and he made a slight nod. This was enough for Lucius. He reached up to his face and began scraping away the false nose and scar. They crumbled away quite easily in his hands. The woman's expression didn't change as his face was revealed. Demetrius continued to stare into the middle distance.

'My name is Lucius Valerius Aquila,' he said, and it felt good, after so long, to be able to say it out loud. 'This is my brother, Quintus, and this is our friend Isidora. Quintus and I are the sons of Aquila, the senator who was murdered seven months ago. The day before he was killed, my father was at the Flavian family villa in Aquae Cutiliae where he witnessed –'

'The murder of Titus,' finished Claudia.

'You know the truth, then,' said Lucius, relief flooding through him.

She nodded, colour entering her cheeks for the first time. 'And you do, too, by the sound of it!' she said.

'How do you know he was murdered?' asked Isi.

'My husband cared for the emperor in his final hours,' answered Claudia. 'He immediately suspected that Titus had been poisoned. We have a well-stocked

---

* *chorus: a group of performers who comment on the action in a Greek or Roman play.*

library here, and I often used to read to my husband in the evenings. As he sat there by the emperor's side, observing his suffering, he recalled a work I once read to him by Nicander of Colophon, an expert on poisons. My husband realised that Titus was exhibiting the exact symptoms Nicander had attributed to the poison belladonna – fever, dry mouth, rapid pulse, dilation of pupils, headaches. Later, when he performed the autopsy on the emperor, his suspicions were confirmed. He found belladonna seeds in his stomach.'

Lucius's heart skipped a beat. Here was proof – official proof from the emperor's own physician – that Titus had been murdered. While Claudia had been talking, a new plan had begun forming in his mind. Perhaps they wouldn't need to kill Glabrio. If they could prove he murdered Titus, he'd be executed, and then honour could be restored to their family.

'And your husband recorded his findings in his report?' he asked.

'Yes,' said Claudia. 'But when he showed the report to Consul Glabrio, the consul burned it.'

Burned it! Lucius's brief surge of hope now plummeted.

'And why do you suppose Glabrio did that?' demanded Quin, frustration evident on his face.

Claudia looked hard at him, seemingly surprised by the question. 'I always assumed it was for political reasons,' she said, 'to protect the new emperor. If it had emerged that Titus had been murdered, people would have immediately suspected Domitian – whether he was behind it or not…'

'So who do you think murdered Titus?' probed Quin.

'I have no idea,' said Claudia, looking somewhat affronted by his aggressive questions. 'If you know, sir, please enlighten me…'

'It was Glabrio,' sighed Lucius.

'Glabrio?' Claudia paled. 'I half suspected, but how… how do you know?'

'When my father and his friend were in the emperor's villa, they found the cook dying in the kitchen. Before he died he told them that Glabrio had stabbed him in order to ensure his silence…'

'Silence about what?'

'About the fact that Glabrio had ordered him to poison the emperor's food.'

Claudia's hand moved to her cheek. 'It's all starting to make horrid sense,' she whispered. 'So that's why your father was killed…'

Lucius nodded. 'All we want is justice and honour for our father…'

'And to kill Glabrio,' added Quin.

'The evidence your husband gathered may help us,' said Lucius. 'At least, I hoped it might. But now you say Glabrio destroyed the report?'

She nodded. 'I'm afraid he did. My husband could only watch as he threw it onto the fire. Then Glabrio asked him to write a second version, stating that Titus died of a fever. As Diomedes told it to me later, the consul persuaded him it was in Rome's best interests. He said that if the truth ever came out there would be an uprising. The regime could fall, leading to chaos and bloodshed. That's what the consul said, apparently. But now I'm not so sure it happened that way. I think my husband was protecting me from the truth. If Glabrio really was trying to cover up his own crime, then I'm sure he used threats rather than persuasion. He probably threatened my husband with death – my death and the death of our children. That would make more sense. You see, Diomedes loved the truth. He loved it with a passion. He wouldn't have lied in a report just because Glabrio told him it was politically necessary. Only threats to those he loved would have persuaded him. In the end, he recorded that Titus had died of a fever caused by swamp fumes – *miasma*, to use the technical term. It was complete nonsense. I can't imagine how painful it must have been for him to write.' Claudia dabbed an eye with her sleeve.

'Madam,' said Quin gently, 'I'm sorry for what you've had to go through. And I thank you for sharing your story with us. Now at least you know why your husband was killed, and we know that our father was right about the murder. But I don't see where we can go from here. We've reached a dead end. All the witnesses to Glabrio's crimes are now dead, and the original autopsy report is destroyed. There's nothing more we can do.'

'Are you sure about that?' said Claudia, and Lucius glimpsed something in her expression that gave him a tingle of encouragement.

'Unless...' began Isi.

Claudia looked at her. 'Unless?' she prompted.

'Unless there's another copy of the original report,' said Isi.

A smile crept onto Claudia's face. 'You've guessed it, my dear! My husband made a second copy, which Glabrio knew nothing about.'

Lucius tried to keep his excitement under control. *So all was not lost!*

'He kept it here, in the tablinum, opposite a bust of Titus,' said Claudia. 'It was as if he wanted the emperor to know that the truth about his death had not been forgotten, and would one day be revealed. Unfortunately, he mentioned all this to a friend. That was a mistake. The man turned out not to be a friend after all. He must have gone straight to Glabrio. When the Praetorian guards arrived, Diomedes was in the tablinum. He immediately guessed why they had come and he told Demetrius to hide the autopsy report. You hid it out here in the garden, didn't you, Demetrius?'

'Yes, my lady.'

Lucius surveyed the shrubs around him, wondering where the steward might have concealed the report. There was no obvious hiding place. He prayed it had not been found and destroyed.

'Where did you hide it?' he asked Demetrius, trying

to remain calm.

'Should I tell them, my lady?'

'Yes, Demetrius.'

'I hid it in the urn.'

Claudia smiled, patting the Grecian urn that stood on a plinth next to her bench. 'The Praetorians searched everywhere,' she said. 'They made a complete mess of the house. But clever Demetrius fooled them. They never thought to look in here.'

Lucius stared at the urn. 'So is it still in there?'

Claudia shook her head sadly, and continued with her story: 'The following morning, my husband left the house to call on a patient – a senator who lives on the other side of the hill. He never made it. The next time I saw him was yesterday, at the Temple of Libitina, where I went to identify his body... But going back to the day he disappeared – I feared the worst. I thought they might have captured him and were torturing him to make him tell them where the report was. I tried to think what he would have wanted me to do in these circumstances, and I realised that, above all, he would want the truth preserved. In other words, I had to ensure the survival of the report. I decided to send it far away from here. I entrusted it to Parmenion, my husband's scribe, who was only too glad to leave. Being privy to all my husband's writings, he was convinced that the Praetorians would come for him next. The only question was where to send him. Luckily, Demetrius came to our rescue once again. He suggested that Parmenion join the army. As a former centurion of the Twentieth Valeria Victrix,* Demetrius was able to write him a letter of recommendation.'

'The Twentieth,' said Quin. 'They're based in Britannia, aren't they?'

'Yes, sir,' said Demetrius, a tremor of emotion entering his voice for the first time. 'Commanded by General Agricola. They're currently engaged in the conquest of Caledonia.'**

'He has the report with him, I suppose?' muttered a thoughtful Quin.

Claudia gave a pained shrug. 'I can only hope so. I told him to guard it with his life.'

'Caledonia…' Quin spoke the word as if it were the name of a mythical land, which it almost was. 'That's in the far north of Britannia, yes?'

'Indeed,' said the steward.

Lucius clenched his fists with frustration. So the report they needed to destroy Glabrio was now somewhere on the wildest and most northerly frontier of the empire – about as far from Rome as it was possible to get!

---

* *Twentieth Valeria Victrix: a legion of the Roman army, stationed in Britannia (Britain). Its name means 'Victorious Valerian Legion'.*

** *Caledonia: the Roman name for Scotland.*

CHAPTER II

22–23 APRIL

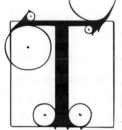he cellar beneath the abandoned tavern was a gloomy, windowless space of brick pillars, damp walls, arched recesses and piles of amphorae* where the occasional rat could be seen scurrying. Against one of the walls rose a steep staircase with a weathered oak-and-iron door at the top. There were straw mats for beds in the alcoves and an ancient table and some three-legged stools in the centre of the room. A couple of oil lamps cast a desultory glow across the table where Lucius, Isi and Quin had gathered to discuss their next move.

Lucius spoke for them all when he said: 'I suppose we must go to Britannia, track down Parmenion and get hold of this report.'

* amphorae: earthenware jars with pointed ends, used for wine and other goods.

The idea made Isi laugh. 'I may be the first Egyptian ever to visit that remote island.' Then, after surveying their squalid surroundings, she added: 'But I agree, it would be good to get out of Rome. I'm sick of living like a rat.'

'Our best hope of finding Parmenion would be to join the Twentieth Legion ourselves,' said Quin, who was busy sharpening his gladius* with a leather strap. 'That way we can get inside the fortified camps and start asking people where he is.'

'And how am I, an Egyptian girl, ever going to be allowed to become a Roman legionary?' asked Isi.

'You managed to become a gladiator,' Quin pointed out.

'That was different and you know it,' said Isi. 'We were travelling from place to place – it was much easier to pretend to be someone else. Besides, the world of gladiators is a lot more informal than the army. We're bound to face serious questions…'

'We can disguise you – give you a new identity.'

'I think you overestimate your abilities in that area, Quintus Felix,' said Isi. 'If Claudia could see we were wearing make-up, then recruiting officers at a legionary camp most definitely will.'

'What do you think, Lu?' asked Quin.

'I think Isi has a point,' said Lucius. 'It'll be very hard for her to get through the selection process. As for you and me, we're probably the two most wanted

* *gladius: Roman infantry sword.*

people in Rome right now…'

'Yes, but not in Britannia,' interjected Quin. 'Glabrio might have the Praetorians eating out of his palm, but the Twentieth Legion is a different matter. General Agricola won't give a fig about who we are, as long as we can fight.'

'How can you be so sure of that?' Isi challenged him.

Quin stopped his sharpening and looked them both in the eye. 'I was in the Forum yesterday,' he said. 'The Senate crier* said that Agricola was planning a big push against the Caledonians in the next few weeks. The Twentieth are bound to be looking for new recruits, and they won't look too closely when three willing and able youths show up at their door, all of us very capable with our swords… If we can get Demetrius to help us with a letter of rec–'

He never finished the word, for at that moment the door at the top of the stairs crashed open.

Lucius jerked backwards as a shadow filled the doorway. Quin stood up, knocking over his stool. His sword glittered in the lamplight. Fearful thoughts about what must have happened crowded into Lucius's brain. They'd been discovered! Glabrio must have found the message and forced Val to translate it. Now the soldiers were here…

But then he took a closer look at the figure loping

---

* *Senate crier: the official who summoned senators to meetings of the Senate, the ruling council of ancient Rome.*

down the stairs and his fear turned to joy as he recognised the long, hairy limbs, the big, round, grey-furred muzzle and heavy brows of Simio, his sister's tame chimpanzee.

'Oooh oooh ah ah ah!' the chimp cried as he swung himself down from one of the lower steps to land lightly on his feet.

'Simio!' they all cried, rushing to greet him.

Lucius gave him a hug. 'You clever, clever boy,' he said. 'You found us!'

Simio panted and grunted excitedly, waving a papyrus note he had clutched in one of his hands.

Quin grabbed the note, then frowned. 'It's the exact same message you lobbed through the window yesterday morning,' he said.

'Turn it over,' suggested Isi.

Quin did so. 'Ah, yes,' he said, studying the squiggles written on the reverse. 'It must be a return message from Val. Looks like the same sort of gibberish that you wrote. What does it say, Lu?' He handed it to his brother.

The words, written in a hurried scrawl on the paper, were as follows:

L zloo eh pɗnlqj ɗq riihulqj ɗw wkh Whpsoh ri Yhqxv Jhqhwula lq wkh Iruxp ri Fɗhvɗu wrpruurz ɗiwhuqrrq ɗw qrɗ krɗ. Y

Lucius saw at once that she'd used the same code as he had. It was based on one his father had once taught him

– known as the 'Caesar cipher' because Julius Caesar had apparently used it in private correspondence. Each letter was replaced by the letter three places further on in the alphabet, so A became D, B became E, and so on. It took Lucius no more than a few minutes to translate the message. 'She says she'll be making an offering at the Temple of Venus Genetrix in the Forum of Caesar tomorrow afternoon at nona hora,'* he said.

'Then one of us must go there and meet her,' said Quin.

'But how?' asked Isi. 'She's bound to be accompanied by Glabrio or one of his guards.'

Quin picked up one of the apricots they'd bought at the Forum Holitorium that morning and tossed it to Simio, who caught it expertly in his mouth. 'We'll think of something,' he said.

The Temple of Venus Genetrix was situated in the Forum of Caesar, to the northeast of the Forum Romanum. Lucius approached it furtively, moving through the thickest parts of the crowd that had gathered in the city centre to witness the public speeches and criminal trials. As always, there were groups of eagle-eyed Praetorians about, so he kept his head down and tried to look anonymous.

The temple had been damaged in the fire that had

---

* *nona hora: the ninth hour of the day (early afternoon).*

swept through Rome two years earlier, and as he came closer Lucius could see that part of it remained covered in scaffolding. From his history studies, he recalled that the temple had been built by Julius Caesar in the year 707 AUC* following his victory over his rival Pompey at the Battle of Pharsalus in Greece. Venus Genetrix was the goddess of motherhood and also the mother of Aeneas, who was believed to be the ancestor of Caesar's family, the Julii.

The front of the temple was an impressive sight, with its eight marble columns supporting a pediment** dense with intricate relief carvings. The temple was raised on a high platform or podium and could only be entered by one of two narrow staircases built into its sides. Lines of worshippers were progressing slowly up both staircases. Today was the annual wine festival – Vinalia Urbana – and as Venus was a patron deity of wine, people were flocking to her temples to make their offerings and sacrifices.

Lucius joined one of the queues, wishing he'd brought along some myrtle, mint or wine so as to appear like any other devotee of the goddess. According to the sundial he had passed in the Forum, it was not yet nona hora, but he looked around for Valeria in case she'd arrived early. He couldn't see her anywhere.

* AUC: short for ab urbe condita ('since the foundation of the city'). Most Romans believed that the city was founded in 753 BC, so 707 AUC comes to 46 BC in the Christian calendar.

** pediment: a long, low triangular panel at the end of a roof.

The line he was in eventually snaked between the pillars and through the entrance into the cool, dim interior of the temple. The main room, known as the cella, was dominated by a giant statue of Venus, raised on a podium at the back. It was flanked by a statue of Caesar and a golden one of the Egyptian queen Cleopatra. Panels in the richly veined marble walls contained Greek paintings of cherubs representing Eros, son of Venus, and the wine god Dionysus. The aroma of incense and the lilting sounds of flute and lyre added to the hallowed ambience. Someone ahead of Lucius in the queue pointed to an armoured breastplate in an alcove on the right-hand side. 'Caesar's own armour!' he said in awed tones to his companion. 'See those pearls set into the bronze decoration – they come from Britannia.'

Lucius gazed at the impressive relic. *Was this a sign?* The mysterious, mist-covered northern isle seemed to be calling to him. While he was contemplating this, his eye was caught by a tall figure standing in the line near the breastplate. From the armed lictors* positioned around him, Lucius could tell at once that he was important. Then, with a shudder, he recognised the narrow face, high cheekbones, hooded eyes and long, hooked nose: Glabrio!

Fearing that he might be seen by the man or his lictors, Lucius hastily ducked behind the people in front of him. He peered from behind the headdress

* *lictors: the bodyguards of a Roman magistrate.*

of an amply proportioned lady and caught sight of his mother standing next to the consul. Just behind them stood Valeria, with her own personal lictor standing guard over her.

It was the first time Lucius had laid eyes on his sister since that terrible day on the Via Appia seven months ago when he'd watched her get captured. She was staring straight ahead, so didn't see him. He noticed that she had grown taller, and her girlish prettiness was maturing into real beauty. Yet there were shadows of sadness around her eyes and a weariness in her posture that alarmed him. She was a caged bird, he guessed – living in luxury, but essentially a prisoner. The presence of the lictor reinforced this impression. Why did she need a personal guard? Did Glabrio think she might try to escape – or that someone might try to rescue her?

His mother had her humble, devout face on – the one she always wore on temple visits. Yet she seemed happy and relaxed, he thought, and standing rather too close to Glabrio for his liking. Lucius prayed that she was no more than a house guest of the consul's. If their relationship had become more than that, it would complicate everything.

The three of them, and their lictors, were in a line on the right-hand side of the temple, which was moving very slowly towards the marble altar that stood in front of the statue of Venus, where offerings were made. Each of them was carrying a small flask of wine and some sprigs of myrtle. Lucius was in another line on the left-hand side, which was progressing in the same direction at a similarly slow pace. He looked helplessly towards Val. The lictor never moved from her side. Lucius realised he had absolutely no chance of communicating with her without the lictor or Glabrio, who was standing just in front of her, knowing about it. He would have to think of something else.

The one advantage they had, he realised, was that only Val was expecting to see him. He saw her subtly eyeing the people around her, barely moving her head as she did so. It was no good, though – she would have to turn her head ninety degrees to have any chance of spotting him, and she couldn't do that without the lictor noticing.

Lucius looked ahead, towards the back of the temple, where a worshipper was kneeling before the altar. This, he realised, was the one moment when each visitor to the temple was alone – well, almost alone: the sacerdos, or temple priest, stood nearby on the podium. As was customary, the priest's head was entirely covered by his toga to guard against sights and sounds of ill omen. If only Lucius could be that priest when Val came up to make her sacrifice… He'd be able to talk to her and no one would know it was him. But how could he take the man's place?

Lucius watched the priest carefully for the next five minutes. At one stage he saw him move behind a screen at the rear of the podium, to the left of the

Venus statue. When the priest emerged a short while later, he seemed just a little unsteady on his feet. If his face had been visible at that moment, Lucius was sure his cheeks would look flushed. The man had clearly helped himself to some of the temple wine.

That was when the idea occurred to Lucius. It was incredibly – stupidly – risky, but what choice did he have? This might be his only chance of communicating with his sister, and he wasn't going to pass it up. In a fold of his toga, Lucius carried a small flask of valerian-root potion. Isi had mixed it up for him yesterday because he was having trouble getting to sleep. He'd put a few drops of it into some water last night and it had sent him off into the arms of Somnus* almost immediately.

Without waiting to reflect on the sheer foolhardiness of his plan, Lucius ducked out of the line of worshippers and began edging his way towards the back of the temple. The press of bodies hindered his progress, but also paradoxically helped him, for in the confusion of people moving in and out of the temple he was able to duck and weave his way past others without their noticing. When he reached the podium, he slipped behind the statue of Caesar and peered out. He saw that the priest was busy helping a worshipper with her libation,** so he was able to steal behind the screen at the back without being noticed.

* *Somnus: god of sleep.*

** *libation: an offering of oil or wine.*

As expected, he found a little table there supporting a silver flagon of dark red wine. Lucius uncorked his flask and tipped half of the valerian-root decoction into the wine. To judge from the effects of just a few drops of the stuff on himself, he reckoned he'd poured enough in to knock the priest out for a few hours at least.

After recorking his flask, Lucius sidled out from behind the screen and crept into the opposite corner of the temple, shielded from general view by the great plinth of the statue of Venus and the smaller statue of Cleopatra. Here he waited, hoping that the priest would decide to take one more secret swig before Val took her turn on the podium.

From his position, he could see Val and her party drawing ever closer to the front of the queue. Soon it was Glabrio's turn to make his sacrifice. The man's hard expression did not grow softer in the presence of the goddess, nor did his cold eyes grow warmer. He carried out the rituals and spoke the words in the correct manner, but it was all very perfunctory and without feeling. When he was finished, the consul rose to his feet and descended from the podium, and then it was Caecilia's turn to approach.

Time was running out! Lucius heard the priest make a smacking sound with his lips. Was he getting thirsty?... It appeared not. He remained stubbornly where he was.

Caecilia performed the rites more slowly than

Glabrio, and with more obvious emotion. The flute and the lyre continued their pious, formless melodies, and Lucius strained to hear his mother's murmured words to Venus Genetrix as she knelt by the altar: 'Goddess of motherhood,' he heard her say, 'in offering this calpar* I humbly beg that you will be gracious and merciful to me, to my house and household, to my daughter Valeria and to my son Lucius, wherever he may be. I pray that you keep him safe…'

Did she mean it, he wondered sadly. Did she really care about him?

He watched her pour the libation into a shallow bowl. In accordance with tradition, this was wine from a cask filled last September, now opened for the first time. Lucius brushed a tear from his cheek as the thought struck him: when that wine had last been exposed to air, they had been living in their house on the Esquiline Hill. His father had been alive…

'Oh Venus, goddess of love,' Caecilia continued, 'I pray that you look with kindness upon my forthcoming marriage to Marcus Glabrio. I hope that you will bless our union and grant us happiness in the years to come.'

Lucius almost gasped out loud when he heard these words fall from her lips. How could she? He wanted to run to his mother, seize her by the shoulders and tell her the truth about the man she planned to wed and the crimes he had committed. Their marriage could

---

* *calpar: pitcher of wine.*

not go ahead. Glabrio could *not* become part of their family! Somehow, she had to be warned. His mother would assume he was lying, of course – but Val would believe him, and she might have some influence on their mother. He simply had to speak to Val. But the priest was still standing there, stubbornly refusing to drink the wine.

Caecilia completed her prayers. She laid a sprig of myrtle in the pewter dish, rose to her feet and returned to where Glabrio was waiting for her. Lucius watched Val ascend to the podium, leaving her lictor at the foot of the steps. She looked furtively around, as if hoping to see Lucius somewhere. He was just a few short paces away, cloaked in shadow. But the guard's eyes were fixed on her, and so were Glabrio's. If Lucius came out and spoke to her now, it might be the last thing he ever did.

As Val knelt before the altar, the priest retreated a few steps and decided – at last! – to slip behind the screen. Lucius pressed himself further back into the shadows so the priest wouldn't see him. He watched the man draw back his hood and raise the flagon to his lips. He was a portly fellow with a large head and the ruddy complexion of a seasoned drinker. This made Lucius worry that there might not be enough potion in there to affect him. He took a sip and some of the wine dribbled down his fat chin. He wiped it away quickly before it could stain his toga. Then he took a much bigger glug.

Lucius waited, the tension rising within him. Nothing happened. The priest returned the flagon to the table and replaced his hood, readying himself for his return to the podium. As he emerged from behind the screen, he stopped and wobbled slightly. He took another hesitant step forward, then staggered a little. Perhaps he guessed that something was wrong, for he suddenly rushed back behind the screen as if anxious not to embarrass himself in full view of the worshippers. He pushed back his hood, rubbed his eyes, blinked and swayed. Then he slowly collapsed against the rear wall, sliding down until his bottom hit the marble floor and his feet poked out from beneath the screen.

As quickly as he could, Lucius rushed over to the fallen priest and pushed his feet out of sight. He grabbed the man's toga in both hands and pulled it hard so that the whole thing unravelled from his body at speed, making the body roll several times across the floor. Lucius grabbed hold of his arm just as the unconcious priest was about to roll into full view of everyone in the temple. He yanked him back behind the screen. After shrugging off his own toga praetexta,* Lucius began to dress himself in the priest's larger toga virilis.** He wrapped the material around himself, taking care over the folds, and finally pulling the back part over his

* *toga praetexta: a white toga with a purple stripe, worn by freeborn boys and magistrates.*

** *toga virilis: a plain white toga worn by men who were not magistrates.*

head like a hood, as the priest had done. When he was sure his head was completely covered, Lucius took a deep breath and stepped out from behind the screen. He was relieved to see that Val was still kneeling at the altar saying her prayers.

He moved slowly towards her, head bowed as he'd seen the priest do – conscious of everyone's eyes on him. Had they noticed that the priest had suddenly grown taller and thinner? To his relief, there were no sounds of surprise – just the usual mutterings and murmurings of those waiting their turn.

Val was now on her feet, preparing to make her libation. As she raised her flask, Lucius placed his hand on hers. She looked up curiously. 'Let me help you, my child,' he said in a voice loud enough to be heard by her lictor, who was still standing at the base of the podium. Lucius slowed down her hand, so that the wine trickled rather than poured from the flask. 'It's me,' he whispered. The music, he hoped, was just about loud enough to mask the sound of his voice to anyone but her.

He heard her suppress a gasp. Her hand shook once, very slightly, causing some wine to spill outside the bowl. Then she steadied herself and replied equally softly: 'Lucius?'

'Glabrio killed Father,' he breathed.

He felt her muscles straining just to stay in control. His hand tightened on hers in case she dropped the flask. Her voice was little more than a stifled sob: 'He's going to marry Mother.'

'You have to stop the wedding.'

The flask was almost empty. Her sprig of myrtle had already been laid. He would have to find some other reason for delaying her here. As the last of the wine dripped into the bowl, Lucius racked his brain for something to say or do, but couldn't think of anything.

Then Val came to his rescue. 'Oh dear,' she exclaimed in a loud voice. 'I think I said the prayer wrong earlier, when you weren't here, Sacerdos. I'll have to do it again. Could you just check that I say the words correctly this time?'

'Of course,' he said.

Someone coughed behind them – it was a discreet sound, yet definitely impatient. Lucius guessed it was Glabrio, wanting to be gone.

Val ignored it and began to chant: 'Venus Genetrix, charmer of gods and mankind, nurturing mother, beneath the starry signs that glide through the night, You enliven the ship-bearing seas and the fruitful earth, since it is through you that all things are conceived and animated into life to behold the light of day…' She trailed off. 'Do you have proof… that he did it?' she whispered.

'The proof is with a scribe travelling with the legions in Britannia,' he murmured. Then, more loudly, he said: 'Very good, my child. Now, please continue.'

'Goddess,' Val recited, 'for you the winds make way, the heavenly clouds open at your coming, the miraculous earth greets you with sweet-scented flowers, for you the surface of the sea laughs, and the peaceful heavens glisten in luminescence...' Her voice dropped once more to a whisper: 'You must go to Britannia and get the proof. Whatever you do, get out of Rome. If you stay here even one day longer, you will be caught...'

There came another cough, louder this time. Lucius glanced behind and saw that the lictor had placed his foot on the first step that led up to the podium. Behind him, Glabrio was visibly twitching as he glared at them. The worshippers waiting behind them were also looking annoyed at how long she was taking.

He turned back to his sister and saw once again the sad resignation in her eyes – it was a terrible thing to see in a girl so young, who had once been so full of life and hope. 'Wait for us,' he murmured, taking her hand once more. 'We'll come back for you, I promise.'

Val tried to smile. 'Together forever,' she mouthed. It was something Quin had once said – two simple words that had become a mantra for the three of them. He hoped she still believed it.

They both rose to their feet and she was about to leave him when there came a crash from the back of the podium. Lucius turned to see that the screen had fallen to the ground, revealing the priest in his tunic, who was struggling to rise to his feet.

There were gasps of shock around the temple as the worshippers took in this sight. Lucius decided it was time he made his escape. Before anyone else could react, he leapt off the podium and began forcing his way through the packed cella towards the front entrance. Behind him, Glabrio's shrill voice stabbed the air: 'Seize him! Seize the imposter!' The iron-shod sandals of the lictors echoed on the marble floor tiles as they made their way towards him, but they were as hampered as Lucius by the crush of bodies.

Unable to make progress on his feet, Lucius got down on his knees and crawled and squeezed his way through a forest of legs towards the sunlit rectangle of the entrance. He barged through the final congregants and burst out into the Forum of Caesar. Without breaking stride, he sprinted to his right towards the portico that surrounded the forum. He ran beneath the colonnade until he came to an exit. This led him down a narrow alley to the Clivus Lautumiarum, the busy road that led back to the Forum Romanum. It was easier here to blend into the crowds, but he couldn't risk slowing down. He could hear the shouts and pandemonium in his wake as his pursuers pushed pedestrians aside in their efforts to catch up with him. In fact, he didn't stop running until he reached the tavern refuge. Panting for breath, he swung open the front door just as booted feet clattered into the Forum Holitorium behind him. He cursed his fate – they'd kept pace with him. Lucius ran down the cellar steps before flinging himself onto his mattress.

'They've found us,' he wheezed to Isi and Quin,

who had risen from the table where they'd been eating lunch.

'Are they upstairs?' asked Quin, reaching for his gladius.

'Not yet,' said Lucius, swallowing to get his breath back under control. 'They're in the Forum Holitorium. But the locals have seen us come in and out of this place enough times. It won't take the guards long to get the information out of them. We've got ten minutes at most.'

'Then we'd better get out of here,' said Isi. 'There's a back way out of the tavern upstairs. Come on!' She grabbed her bag of treasured possessions and began mounting the steps.

'Where do we go now?' cried Lucius, struggling to his feet. 'We can't just keep running.'

'We'll go to Britannia – join the Twentieth,' said Quin. He held up a parchment scroll. 'Isi went and got this for us this morning. It's a letter of recommendation from Demetrius.'

Lucius stared at it, and gulped.

'Your name's Lucius Galerius Tertius,' smiled Quin, 'and I'm your brother, Quintus Galerius Maximus. Get used to it!'

'Hurry!' yelled Isi from the top of the steps.

'Who's she?' Lucius asked.

'She's your other brother, Amulius Galerius Cato,' said Quin, tying on his sword belt.

'So she's wise, you're the greatest, and I'm… third,'* grumbled Lucius. 'This is the last time I'm going to let either of you do the renaming thing, OK?'

'OK!' laughed Quin. 'Now come on!'

Lucius grabbed his knife, a loaf of bread and the last of the nectarines, and followed his brother up the stairs.

---

* *wise, greatest, third: Cato was a famous Roman philosopher of the 1st century BC; maximus is Latin for 'greatest'; tertius means 'third'.*

PART TWO

CALEDONIA

CHAPTER III

20 MAY

Lucius had rarely felt so exhausted. Every muscle in his body burned as he followed Quin and Isi up the steep, winding track. The land around them had a stark beauty, like nothing he'd ever seen in Italy or in any of his travels around the Mediterranean. But the wind bit like a knife, and the rain – the constant misty rain – soaked him to the bone. If that wasn't enough, his stomach ached for want of food. For days they'd eaten nothing but nuts, berries and mushrooms, supplemented by the occasional small animal or fish they'd managed to catch. What he wouldn't give right now for a bowl of meat stew from his favourite popina* back in Suburra…

Finally, they reached the summit of the hill. As Lucius leaned against a rocky outcrop and caught his breath, he heard the other two gasp. He opened his eyes and was confronted by a spectacular sight: the landscape had opened up before them to the north. They were standing on the crest of a ridge, which descended steeply towards a green valley over four hundred feet** below. Through this valley meandered a river, which must have originated in the great mountains visible on the far horizon. The rain had eased off, and a shaft of pale sunlight lanced through the stormclouds, brightening a swathe of the valley grass and making it golden. High above them, an eagle circled.

For a moment none could speak, each dumbstruck by the majesty of the sight. Then Quin shouted: 'There it is!' Lucius squinted in the direction he was pointing and saw, some four miles*** away across the valley, plumes of blue smoke rising from a heavily wooded plateau in the crook of one of the river's many bends. It had to be their destination: the legionary fortress of Pinnata Castra.**** Or so they hoped! It was hard to be sure from this distance.

* *popina: fast-food restaurant.*

** *400 Roman feet = about 120 metres.*

*** *4 Roman miles = about 6 km.*

**** *Pinnata Castra: a Roman fort at present-day Inchtuthil, Tayside, Scotland. Its name probably means 'the fortress on the wing'.*

Their last experience of Roman civilisation had been at Cataractonium,* a military fortress with a vicus, or civilian settlement, attached to it. That had been 150 miles** to the south. And it hadn't been that civilised in truth, lacking even a bathhouse to wash off the filth of travel. They'd spoken to some off-duty soldiers in the tavern there, members of the Ninth Legion, but none had heard of Parmenion. The soldiers had directed them north to the fort of Pinnata Castra, here in the land of the Venicones tribe. They said it was currently serving as the advance headquarters of General Agricola, and the Twentieth were based there.

Since leaving Cataractonium, Lucius, Quin and Isi had spent days walking through increasingly strange and savage landscapes: dark, dripping forests and wind-blasted moors. They'd camped in ravines and forest clearings, and lit fires to keep the wolves at bay. They'd forded rushing streams of icy water where Lucius had once managed to spear a salmon with his knife as it leapt upriver. Sometimes they passed close to primitive villages of round grass huts – round, Lucius guessed, because it was the best shape for any building in such a wind-cursed land. Occasionally they would glimpse the natives: fierce, flame-haired people with painted faces, moving amid the misty, boulder-strewn uplands. In the last day or so, their route had taken them past a few small fortlets guarding river and

* *Cataractonium: present-day Catterick, North Yorkshire.*

** *150 (Roman) miles = about 220 km.*

73

estuary valleys. But the garrisons there had offered little or no hospitality – only reassurance that they were on the right track.

Now here they were, hungry, exhausted – and close, surely!

'Come on!' said Quin, starting down the hillside. 'If we hurry, we'll be at the castra in time for lunch!'

A sharp whistling sound split the air above them, and blood erupted from Quin's shoulder. Lucius watched, stunned, as his brother tipped forward and rolled and bounced down the hill. His head collided with a boulder and he fell still. Before Lucius could react, the air hissed again close to his right ear, and an arrow thudded into the path just one pace away from where he was standing. For a second, Lucius could only stare, mesmerised, at the quivering shaft. Then he was tugged violently backwards into the shelter of the outcrop. He turned to see Isi looking at him, her face tight with tension. They pressed themselves flat against the rough surface of a big, greyish-white granite boulder. She gestured above her with an upward tilt of her head, and held up two fingers. What was she saying? Two, above them – two what? Painted savages, he assumed, on top of the boulder.

The wind had dropped to a low, gusting moan across the hilltop. Lucius could hear his own panicked breath in the crevices of the rock. There was a scraping sound above them, and a trickle of dislodged stones. One or both of the savages were on the move, coming down from their perch to finish them off. Lucius drew his knife. Isi reached into her bag and pulled out a round bronze mirror with an ornate ivory handle – an unlikely weapon! Was she thinking of bartering her way out of this?

With her eyes, Isi indicated for him to slowly circle the rock clockwise. He began to edge his way round, leaving her where she was. He gripped the knife tight, feeling the handle become clammy with his sweat. Any second now, he would come face to face with their attackers, and survival would depend on who had the faster reflexes. After seven months of gladiatorial training, Lucius knew he could be both quick and deadly in the arena, but that probably counted for little in this alien setting. These people knew the landscape. They knew where to hide and where to ambush.

After inching his way around half the circumference of the rock, Lucius stopped. He had yet to see anyone. He saw now that there were other outcroppings close by, sticking out of the rough grass, and the savages could be hiding behind any of these with their arrows aimed at him. Isi had seen two, but there could be more. Lucius swallowed. He wanted to run – a moving target would be harder to hit – but how could he run when he didn't know where these people were? He could be running straight towards them.

A dull thunk from the far side of the rock made him jump. It was followed by a groan of pain. Isi? Had she been hit? Or killed? With Quin unconscious, that left Lucius on his own. He whirled around, suddenly desperate to locate their assailants, but they remained stubbornly out of view. He was about to dash back to Isi when a loud noise stopped the air in his throat: it was a high-pitched whoop, like a war cry. From above came another skittering of stones and a shower of dusty rock grains fell into his hair. Then something very heavy dropped on top of him.

Lucius collapsed beneath the weight and quickly found himself sprawled face down on the ground, a knee crushed into his back. He flailed about with his knife, but both his arms were swiftly rendered immobile, pinned to the ground by a pair of muscular hands. Lucius strained with all his might, managing to raise his head a hand's breadth from the ground. He glimpsed powerful forearms covered in intricate blue curling patterns. His captor bellowed at him in a strange, guttural language, then bashed his head, making his ears ring. The knife was torn from his barely resisting fingers, an arm curled tightly around his neck and he was hauled to his feet. Still dizzy from the blow to his head, Lucius found it hard to stand upright. More incomprehensible words were roared at him and he was dragged to the edge of the hilltop, to a point where the land fell away sharply, almost like a cliff. The rocks, some seventy feet* below, glinted like giants' teeth.

Lucius realised he was to be thrown to his death, and

* *seventy feet: about 21 metres.*

the prospect brought him to his senses. He struggled ferociously against the man's grip, determined not to go meekly to his fate. He could do nothing against the neck hold, so he kicked backwards instead. The heel of his sandal connected with a bare shin, and his captor emitted a soft grunt of pain. There was a momentary weakening of the necklock, and he wriggled free, then turned and punched, all in the same movement. His fist connected with the man's jaw. The blue eyes of the savage opened wide as he rocked backwards. The sheer speed of the attack must have startled him, and Lucius blessed the months of training that had sharpened his reflexes to such a pitch. He saw now that the same strange blue patterns snaked their way across the man's bare torso and face. Red hair stood up from his head in wild strands, and more of it drooped from beneath his nose. Around his neck he wore a pendant with a strange beast carved on it.

The man's shocked face transformed into a grin, and he reached for his sword. As he did so, Lucius pushed him hard in the chest, making him stagger. The grin faded and the wild man charged. Lucius put up his hands to grasp his wrists, but the momentum of the attack pushed him backwards, very close to where the land fell away. The pair became locked in a brutal battle above the precipice, each trying to grab the other and force him over the edge. But the man's superior strength was gradually forcing Lucius backwards, inch by inch, until his heels could no longer feel any turf beneath them. The wind whipped through his woollen cloak. It whined like a pack of hungry dogs. He sensed the yawning emptiness behind him and those toothlike rocks far below. He fought with all his remaining strength, straining to grasp at the man's neck. But the momentum was against him – he could already feel his feet starting to slip…

Then, quite suddenly, all the backward pressure ceased. The man continued to stare at him, but the leering menace had disappeared from his face. Instead he looked almost frightened as his gaze dropped to his chest. Lucius looked, too, and saw the reddened tip of a sword blade emerging just below his ribcage. The savage collapsed like a marionette whose strings had been cut. Lucius was so dazed by this turn of events, he almost forgot he was still in danger. As he felt himself toppling backwards, a hand flew out and grabbed his own. Quin was smiling as he hauled his brother back to safety.

'Thank you!' gasped Lucius.

'You're welcome,' said Quin, yanking his gladius from the dead man's back and wiping the blood off on his cloak. His forehead was cut from his impact with the rock and there was a bloody gash on his left shoulder where the arrow had grazed him. 'Where's Isi?'

'She's…' Lucius's mouth went dry as he remembered her earlier groan. He ran back to the rocky outcrop where he'd left her, picking up his knife as he went, in case the other wild man was still about.

As he neared the rock, Isi emerged from behind it, still carrying her bronze mirror. She was limping and looking a bit bruised, but otherwise intact.

Lucius slowed, relief flooding his lungs. 'Where's the one who attacked you?' he asked.

She jerked a thumb back over her shoulder. 'Dead.'

'You killed him with a… with a mirror?'

Isi leaned back against the rock and paused to get her breath. 'I don't think he'd ever seen his reflection before,' she said, massaging her ankle. 'I'm not sure if he was impressed or horrified. Anyhow, it gave me the chance I needed to strike.'

Lucius looked about him warily, expecting to see others.

'It's all right, there were only two of them,' said Isi. 'If there had been any more, we'd be dead by now.'

'Good work,' he said to her. He wanted to hug her, and would have done once – but these days they were still a little uneasy around each other. It had begun with their quarrel about whether to trust Eprius or not. Isi had been proved right when Eprius turned out to be their enemy, and Lucius had apologised. They were back to being friends again. Yet a tension remained. The bitterness of that quarrel had left a scar on their friendship and Lucius wasn't sure if it would ever heal.

'Good work yourself,' Isi said to him, nodding towards the dead man near the precipice.

'Quin helped me out,' said Lucius.

She looked at Quin. 'Glad to see you're still alive.'

Quin was sitting on a nearby boulder. He'd torn off a piece of his tunic and was wrapping it carefully around his shoulder wound. He smiled up at her. 'I don't die easy, as you may have noticed.'

Lucius noticed he was wearing something around his neck. He went closer and saw that it was the pendant the savage had been wearing, which Quin must have taken a fancy to. He took a closer look. It was made of polished black stone inlaid with silver and green enamel, which formed the outline and interior of a weird, snakelike sea monster.

'It's beautiful,' he said.

'For savages, they're pretty skilful,' agreed Quin.

The wind bit hard suddenly, making them shiver.

'They're also dangerous,' said Isi. 'And we're lucky to be alive. The sooner we get inside the walls of the castra, the better.'

They began making their way down the slope towards the valley. Isi, still hobbling on her tender ankle, took the rear, while Lucius took the lead. It was an easy enough descent, and within twenty minutes they had reached the flatter ground of the valley. A footpath led them through the lush grass towards the river.

'That mirror,' Quin remarked to Isi as they walked. 'Why did you bring it? You don't strike me as the vain type.'

'You're right, I'm not,' said Isi. 'The mirror belonged

to my mother. It's the only memento I have of her. My aunt gave it to me when I was in Egypt.'

'Well, keep it safe,' said Quin. 'It saved your life today.'

As they drew nearer to the wooded plateau, they could see, rising up above the trees, wooden watchtowers, and the glint of armour and spears in the low sun.

'Definitely Pinnata!' said Quin excitedly.

The river, which made an elaborate loop around the wood, was spanned by a simple wooden bridge, wide enough for a wagon and horses. Two sentries stood guard at the entry point to the bridge. They watched, gimlet-eyed, as Lucius, Quin and Isi approached.

'Halt!' one of them ordered when the travellers were still twenty paces away.

'State your purpose!' demanded the other.

There was a nervousness about their manner that, in turn, made Lucius jumpy.

'Is this Pinnata Castra?' asked Quin.

'It is.'

'In that case, we're here to join up. We want to join the Twentieth Legion.'

The sentries conferred with one another for a moment, then ordered them to approach. 'You don't look or sound like Britons, and your Latin is first-rate,' one of sentries commented once the newcomers were standing before them. 'Where are you from?'

'Rome,' said Lucius.

The sentries looked surprised. 'You've come all this way to volunteer?'

'We heard about General Agricola's plans to conquer Caledonia and we wanted to help,' said Quin. He spoke with an enthusiasm that Lucius knew was not entirely feigned – of the three of them he was easily the most excited by the prospect of becoming a legionary.

The sentries nodded, seemingly satisfied. They gave each of them a cursory body search, then checked their shoulder bags. Lucius was obliged to hand over his knife, and Quin his sword. They allowed Quin to keep his pendant, but raised their eyebrows at Isi's mirror. 'Not much call for this sort of thing in a soldier's kit,' one of them said.

'No one's going to mind too much how you look around here, ducky!' chortled the other, a tall fellow with bad skin and a broken nose. He eyed his ugly features in the mirror's polished bronze surface.

'All the same, I'd like to keep it if you don't mind,' said Isi. Lucius admired the way she managed to deepen her voice. If he hadn't known otherwise, he wouldn't have suspected she was a girl.

There was a sigh of wind in the trees and a waterbird screeched somewhere on the river behind them. The sentries, having seemed to relax, became tense again as they looked about them. 'Come across any Caledonians on your way here?' the shorter one asked, his eye falling on Quin's wounded shoulder.

'We had a run-in with a couple of them,' answered Quin.

'Then you're lucky to be alive,' said the sentry. 'We could do with some of your luck around here.' He touched a leather pouch hanging from his neck as if it were an amulet.

'Will you let me have my mirror back?' asked Isi with an edge of impatience in her voice.

The tall sentry continued to contemplate his reflection in it, and squeezed a spot on his chin.

'May as well let the kid have it if he wants it so much,' his companion said. 'We're only supposed to confiscate weapons, and I can't see what harm that little thing can do.'

The mirror was handed back, and the sentries stood aside to let the trio cross the bridge.

'Do you know someone by the name of Parmenion in this camp?' Lucius asked them.

Both men looked blank. 'There are men coming and going all the time,' the tall one said. 'It's impossible to keep track. Best person to ask is Tribune Lurco. He knows everything about everyone in this place.' He winked at his companion as he said this, and the pair exchanged a sour smile. Lucius guessed that this Lurco probably wasn't the most popular man in the camp.

After crossing the bridge, they climbed a steep bank and entered a wooded area. They emerged from here to find, rising up before them, the high wooden walls of Pinnata Castra. The camp was square in plan, with rounded corners. Watchtowers, manned by guards, were placed at each corner and halfway along each side. The walls were surrounded by a series of concentric earthen ramparts and ditches. Each rampart was lined by a fearsome palisade of sharpened stakes. The only approach to the camp was via a narrow path that led to the main gates. As they approached the gates, one of the guards in the watchtower above them ordered them to halt and began barking questions at them. Another ten minutes went by before the gates were opened and they were admitted to the camp.

CHAPTER IV

20 MAY

A soldier escorted them along a wide central street, which he called the Via Principalis,* lined with long rectangular barrack blocks. The interior of the camp buzzed with activity. Lucius saw soldiers practising their drills, carpenters at work constructing some stables, a hunting party returning with a boar on their shoulders, and supply wagons trundling along the street. Through open doorways he caught glimpses of a soldier having a haircut, another having his injured arm treated by a doctor, and two more playing dice. The camp reminded Lucius of a small, well-ordered town – except for the lack of women and children. There was something else different as well: Lucius could only describe it as a kind

---

* *Via Principalis: main street. All Roman army camps had the same basic layout.*

of nervousness. He noticed it in the near-silence of the place, the lack of laughter and the way the eyes of some of the off-duty soldiers followed the newcomers' progress as they walked. Lucius was surprised by this, as the camp seemed very secure and well defended. It was quite unlike the atmosphere he'd experienced at Cataractonium and at other settlements they'd passed further south.

At the centre of the camp stood a large, square building – one of only two Lucius had seen that were made of stone rather than wood. Their escort told them it was the principia, or camp headquarters. As they entered, they saw it was built around a courtyard or parade ground, currently empty. They were led along a corridor past a shrine containing the legionary eagle, a gold statue of the Twentieth Legion's emblem – a running boar – and a recently fashioned bust of Emperor Domitian. After passing a few administrative offices, they were shown into a small room where a short, dark-haired man in a white linen tunic was busy writing at a desk. He looked up as they entered.

'New recruits, sir,' said their escort, barely suppressing a smile. 'Said they've come all the way from Rome to join our general in his quest to subdue the Caledonians.'

The officer didn't appear to find this as funny as the escort did. He stood up from his desk and came closer to them. He began to circle them, examining each in turn. Eventually, he said: 'Very well, thank you, soldier.

You can get back to your duties.' When the guard had departed, he resumed his circling. 'Rome, huh?' he said. 'You've come a long way, you three. We pick up most of our recruits from the province, you know – the more subdued parts anyway, further south.' He raised one side of his mouth in a half-smile. 'So how is our beloved imperial capital these days? Is Consul Glabrio still exerting his iron grip on the city?'

'Life is good there, sir,' said Lucius noncommittally.

'In that case, what brings you here to this cold and dismal outpost – apart from a desire to contribute to the greater glory of the empire?' There was humour behind his sarcasm – Lucius found he couldn't help warming to the man. Then the smile vanished. 'You're not running away from anything, are you?'

'No, sir,' said Quin quickly. 'We're here to serve.'

The officer returned to his desk. He shuffled some documents and became more businesslike. 'My name is Cornelius Verres,' he said. 'I'm the optio in charge of recruitment here at Pinnata. Your timing is good. We're under strength right now, and could certainly do with some fresh, eager young blood.'

Quin flashed an I-told-you-so smile at Lucius and Isi, but his face fell at Verres's next words: 'The general is currently campaigning to the northeast, establishing our control of the region after our recent victory against the Venicones.'

'You mean he's left already?' groaned Quin. 'We won't be joining him?'

Verres smiled indulgently. 'I like your spirit, young man. But we wouldn't be sending you out on the front line, even if the general hadn't departed yet – not without giving you some training first.' He took up a pen, dipped it in some ink and held it poised above a blank birchwood leaf-tablet.* 'So,' he said, 'before we go any further, I'll need some details. You wish to join as auxiliaries, yes?'

'As legionaries, sir,' said Quin.

Verres looked up, surprised. 'Then you're Roman citizens, I take it?'

'Yes, sir,' said Quin.

'I have to admit, I'm impressed,' said Verres, leaning back in his chair and appraising them once again. 'Of all the postings our empire has to offer, I can't think of a more unpleasant one than this, on the northern frontier of Britannia. And yet you, as citizens – educated citizens to judge from your mode of speech – decide, of your own free will, to come out here. It's a rare and uplifting example you set.' He blinked away what might have been a tear before returning his attention to his notes. 'If you want to be legionaries, I'll need a letter of recommendation – preferably from someone high-ranking…'

Quin reached into his sack and drew out the parchment scroll that Demetrius had given them. He

---

* *leaf-tablet: the Romans in Britannia often wrote in ink on very thin sheets of wood, rather than using the wax tablets that were more common in other parts of the empire.*

handed it to Verres. The recruitment officer opened it and gave it a quick scan. When he saw the name of the writer, his eyes lit up.

'Well, well!' he exclaimed. 'Of all the veterans of our legion, I can't think of anyone I'd sooner trust than Centurion Manius Julianus Demetrius of the Third Cohort*...' Then he stopped, and frowned. 'Wait a minute, another recruit pitched up a few weeks ago with a letter of recommendation from Demetrius... Now, who was it?'

'Parmenion?' supplied Lucius eagerly.

'That was the fellow!' cried Verres, slapping the desk. 'Do you know him?'

'Yes, he's a... an old friend,' Lucius improvised. 'Is he here, sir?'

'I'm afraid I have no idea,' said Verres. 'I don't deal with deployments. The person to speak to about that would be Appius Mallius Lurco. He's the military tribune** here at Pinnata. You can meet with him after your probatio***...' He hesitated. 'Or, on the other hand, perhaps it's better if you don't. He, um...' – Verres seemed to be struggling to find the right words – 'well, to be frank, he doesn't take kindly to new recruits barging in with petty requests... Tell you what, why don't I do a little digging myself and let you know

---

* *cohort: a military unit comprising about 480 men, or one-tenth of a legion.*

** *military tribune: a senior officer, above the rank of centurion.*

*** *probatio: an interview for new recruits. New legionaries had to be able to prove that they were Roman citizens.*

what I find out…' He turned back to the letter. 'Now, I see that you all have the same nomen,* so can I assume you are brothers?'

'Yes, sir,' said Quin. 'I'm Quintus. This is Lucius, and this here is Amulius.'

Verres's eye lingered on Isi. 'You look a bit darker than your brothers,' he commented, 'and not typically Italian. Greek perhaps? Or maybe African?'

Lucius could sense Isi bristling, but she said nothing.

Quin tried to laugh it off. 'Amulius is always having to put up with jokes about his parentage, sir. But I assure you, my mother was entirely faithful to my father throughout their marriage. He's as much a Galerius as me and Lucius.'

Verres nodded. 'Considering how you three have made it all the way out here on your own resources, I'm not going to apply stringent background checks in the way I normally would. Your very presence here speaks eloquently enough of your character, not to mention the letter from Demetrius. I'll be satisfied to hear a little about yourselves from your own mouths. So please, tell me something of your family background and your lives until now.'

On the journey, the three of them had cobbled together a potted biography of the Galerii brothers. Quin began to launch into it, but Verres held up his

---

* *nomen: family name. A Roman citizen had three names, and the second of these was the nomen. The boys' real nomen is Valerius; their assumed nomen is Galerius.*

hand. 'No, I've heard enough from you, young man. Let the quiet one say something for a change.' He gestured to Isi. 'Galerius Cato – speak!'

Isi cleared her throat. Lucius knew she had deliberately kept quiet, not wishing to put a strain on her voice. Now she had no choice. In as deep a voice as she could manage, she said: 'Our father and uncle owned a fullery* in Suburra, sir. But our uncle was a bad man. He cheated our father – stole from the business. Then our father died, and we fell on hard times. So we decided to become gladiators. We're fighters, sir. But we've decided we don't want to throw our lives away in the arena. We want to fight for Rome. That's why we're here.'

Verres eyed the scars visible on their legs and arms, including the recent injury to Lucius's leg, picked up during his fight with Eprius – and, of course, Quin's shoulder wound, where fresh blood had soaked through the improvised bandage. 'Admirably concise,' he murmured. 'I suspect there's a lot more to the story you've just told, but I like the fact you've underplayed your suffering. I think you'll fit in well here in the Twentieth. We take pride in our achievements on the battlefield, but we don't brag about them.' He dipped his pen again, and made some more notes on the leaf-tablet. 'Normally at this stage I'd do a physical exam, but I can see you're all fit, if a little exhausted from your journey. You're probably quite hungry, too, I should

* *fullery: laundry.*

imagine. So I propose that we proceed directly to the swearing-in.'

He then called each of them in turn to raise their right hand and swear the Military Oath: 'I swear by Jupiter, Mars and Minerva* that I will follow my commander wherever he may lead me. I will obey orders enthusiastically and without question. I accept the power of my commanders to put me to death without trial for disobedience or desertion. I promise to serve under the standards for my allotted time of duty and not to leave before my commander discharges me. I will serve Rome faithfully, even at the cost of my life.'

Quin spoke the words with pride and commitment. Lucius tried to do likewise, but couldn't help worrying about the freedoms they were giving up. They had come here to find Parmenion and get hold of the original autopsy report – yet here they were signing away their lives for the next twenty-five years. How had this happened? Isi, too, looked uneasy as she repeated the phrases. Lucius guessed it must really stick in her throat to swear by gods she did not believe in, and to promise to serve an empire that she actually despised. Silently he thanked her, knowing that she was doing all this out of her friendship for him.

The swearing-in over, Verres made a note of their distinguishing features, including scars – 'so we can identify your corpse on the battlefield,' he explained

---

* *Jupiter, Mars and Minerva: the father of the gods, the god of war and the goddess of wisdom.*

cheerfully. Then he looked at each of them and grinned. 'Congratulations, boys! You're now soldiers of Rome.'

From Verres's office, they were escorted to the mess hall, which lay just behind the headquarters building. It was almost empty, most legionaries having already eaten their midday meal. As soon as they were seated, they began tearing hungrily into their meal of cold meat, cheese, bread and beer. Shortly afterwards, they were joined by a pair of soldiers lately released from sentry duty.

'So what's the general up to?' Quin asked them conversationally once they had introduced themselves.

'I wish I knew,' one of them scoffed. He was a moon-faced man with a stained tunic, his chin wet from the beer he'd just slurped. 'He took a load of carpenters and engineers along with his fighting cohorts, so I guess he's got plans to build. Fat lot of good it'll do. You can build all the forts you like, you'll never civilise this wasteland.'

'Where's he building these forts?' Lucius asked.

'East and west of here,' said the other soldier. 'He's going to build a chain of them, with Pinnata at its centre.' The man's face shone like old leather and a vivid scar ran diagonally across his cheek. Lucius noticed that he did all his eating with his left arm, while his right hung uselessly by his side. 'The forts will protect our conquests to the south,' he said. 'We've defeated the Venicones – that's the Caledonian tribe of this region – but there are other, fiercer tribes not far away. You've seen those big mountains to the north?'

Lucius nodded.

'That's where the danger lies.' He used his teeth to tear off several chunks of his bread, which he then spat out and arranged in a line in front of his plate. 'These are the mountains, you follow me? And between them are these narrow valleys.' He indicated the spaces between the lumps of bread. 'The valleys are the vulnerable points, and that's where the barbarians are likely to attack us from.' With his thumb and forefinger, he broke off some lumps of cheese, which he placed in front of the gaps between the chunks of bread. 'These are the forts the general's building,' he explained. 'He's placing them at the entrances to the valleys to deter the invaders. And he's connecting them up with roads and signal stations to make a secure frontier.'

'Sounds like a plan,' said Quin.

This provoked a snort of laughter from the moon-faced soldier. 'If you want to make the gods laugh, tell them your plans,' he scoffed. 'These barbarians don't recognise frontiers, just like they don't understand battles. We lay waste to their hill forts and they just melt back into the forests and mountains. Then, when we least expect it, they'll ambush our soldiers in some mountain pass, or raid one of our smaller forts. You attack in one direction, and they come back at you from another. It's like fighting water. So we wall ourselves up in our legionary camps and pretend that we control the surrounding land. We'll never conquer these people – and you know it, Gemellus.'

Lucius was starting to understand the nervousness he'd noticed around the camp – assuming this man's assessment of the situation was correct.

Gemellus, the veteran with the useless arm, smiled at Lucius, Quin and Isi. 'Cornix here is our resident cynic,' he said to them. 'He always forgets that we defeated the Venicones.'

'Dispersed them, maybe,' grunted Cornix, after swigging some more beer. 'Burned a few of their farms and villages. But they'll be back.' He cast a tipsy eye on the newcomers. 'Any of you boys heard of Calgacus?'

Lucius shook his head.

'He's a Caledonian chieftain – quite a formidable bloke if you believe the rumours. From what I've heard, the tribes have united under his leadership. Calgacus has got them all in a rage against their common enemy: us! So far we've only had to deal with them as isolated tribes. But you mark my words: if Calgacus can organise them into one force and they all come pouring out of those valleys together, no chain of forts will be able to stop them. When they come, it'll be like the sea…' He threw his arm violently across the table, scattering his friend's pieces of bread and cheese. 'They'll sweep us right out of Caledonia!'

After their meal, Lucius, Quin and Isi visited the quartermaster, who issued them with their uniform, weapons and kit. Their uniform consisted of a white tunic, a pair of iron-studded caligae,* a brass-plated belt, a brown woollen cloak and an iron helmet. Their body armour was a cuirass or breastplate of metal hoops, worn over their torso and shoulders. Quin's eyes lit up when he saw the weapons, which were superior in quality to anything they'd ever fought with as gladiators. They each received a sharp-edged and beautifully balanced gladius made from high-carbon Spanish steel, a large rectangular shield, a spear and a dagger. They were also given a marching pack – a T-shaped pole to which they could lash their kit, including a patera (an all-purpose cup, cooking pot and food bowl), digging tool and cloak. Finally, they were each given their signaculum – a little lead tablet in a leather pouch for them to wear at all times around their necks as an identification tag. It was stamped with their name and the legion's official seal.

Lucius had to admit that Quin, especially, looked the part of a heroic legionary, with his dashing looks and superb physique. Both Lucius and Isi were shorter and slighter, despite the muscles they'd acquired during their gladiatorial training. But just wearing the

* *caligae: heavy-duty sandals worn by soldiers.*

armour made Lucius feel stronger and more confident.

Their training instructor was a barrel-chested centurion by the name of Gallicus, who had a voice deep and loud enough to be heard across the whole camp.* 'A soldier is useful to nobody until he learns how to walk!' he bellowed. And by walking, he meant marching. During their first afternoon of training, he marched them at least twenty times up and down the Via Principalis, bawling in their ears each time one of them fell even slightly out of step. 'Marching,' he shouted (the man didn't seem able to communicate in any other way), 'is what defines a legionary!'

Whenever Gallicus wasn't watching, Lucius allowed his eyes to roam around the camp, watching the groups of soldiers passing by and wondering whether one of them might be Parmenion. Once they'd finished for the day, Gallicus led them to the parade ground in the principia so they could observe some experienced legionaries going through their drills. 'Watch how they move in neat blocks!' he roared. 'They're like a single, deadly animal! That's what I want you lot to be – part of a single, deadly animal!'

As they were leaving the principia on their way to the mess hall, they passed the praetorium – the officers' quarters – which was the only other stone building in the camp. Verres was standing near the entrance speaking with another officer, who looked to be of

* *across the whole camp: Pinnata Castra covered an area of 21.5 hectares (53 acres).*

senatorial rank. Later, as they were tucking into their evening meal, Verres came over to their table. 'Ah, the Brothers Galerii!' he said with a warm smile. 'I've just spoken to Tribune Lurco about your friend...'

Lucius looked up expectantly. 'Is he here, sir?'

'I'm afraid not,' replied Verres. 'He was with the cohorts accompanying Agricola on his fort-building expedition, so there's no telling when or even whether he'll return. Agricola may decide to station him at one of the newly built forts – and then of course there's always the chance he might get himself killed.'

Lucius tried not to let too much of his disappointment show. 'Thank you for letting us know, sir,' he said, staring at his plate.

'Oh, just one other thing,' said Verres, as he was departing. 'Lurco seemed curious that the three of you should be friends with young Parmenion. I have no idea why. Anyway, he quizzed me a little about you and I told him what I recalled of your story. It seemed to satisfy him, but...' He shifted a little uncomfortably. 'Well, I advise you all to take care. He's not the type of fellow to get on the wrong side of, if you take my meaning.'

After cena,* they retired to their quarters in one of the barrack blocks. They were assigned a dormitory

* *cena: the main meal of the day, eaten in the afternoon.*

and a living room, each measuring no more than two paces by four. They would normally have had to share this tiny space with four other soldiers – but following Agricola's departure, the camp was only about half full, so they had the rooms to themselves. This was fortunate for Isi as it prevented any awkwardness when she was getting changed. Lucius and Quin, at least, knew when it was time to turn and face the wall. Of course she could not join the men in the bathhouse, but she took advantage of their absence there to wash herself with a sponge and a bucket of cold water.

That evening the three of them lay exhausted on their beds and listened to the murmur of soldiers, the snuffles and snorts of camp animals and the distant calls of sentries.

'We came here looking for Parmenion, and now we're legionaries,' said Lucius. 'What in Hades* has happened?'

'Don't worry about it, Lu,' said Quin nonchalantly. 'As soon as we find him and get hold of that report, we'll get out of here and head back to Rome.'

'You make it sound so simple,' said Lucius. 'But don't you remember the oath we took? The penalty for desertion is death!'

'*We* didn't take the oath,' said Quin. 'That was the Galerii brothers.' He rolled over, pulling the blanket tight across his shoulders. 'My advice', he yawned, 'is to get some kip. We're going to face another day of

---

* *Hades: the underworld, the abode of the dead.*

heavy training tomorrow.'

Lucius tried to settle down, but he remained agitated. His thoughts spiralled like vultures, continually swooping down and pecking at him. *What if they never found Parmenion? How could they ever escape this place to continue their search elsewhere? And why was Lurco asking questions about them?*

'Lucius?' whispered Isi. 'Are you awake?'

'You can't sleep either, then?'

'No,' she tittered.

He was glad – suddenly the night felt a little bit less lonely. He could just make out her outline in the bed nearest to his. She was lying on her side looking at him, with her head propped up on her fist.

'You worried?' he asked.

He heard her give a deep sigh. 'I'm kind of wondering what we're doing – what we've done – coming here.'

'It does seem crazy,' agreed Lucius. He waited until he could hear Quin's gentle snores, then continued: 'Sometimes I think that my brother would be happy to forget about Parmenion and the autopsy report and just be a soldier.'

'He's always happiest with a sword in his hand,' said Isi. He heard the smile in her voice and was happy he'd found her in a cheerful mood for once.

'I'm very grateful to you,' he said. 'For coming with us, I mean… Just think, if you and I hadn't bumped into each other back in Carthage, you'd still be swanning

around the Mare Nostrum* with the Swords of Isis…
It makes me feel a bit guilty, sometimes – dragging you
away from your life down there.'

'Who says you dragged me away?' said Isi.

'Well…'

'What makes you think I don't want to be here?'

There was a challenge in her voice. Isi always liked
to challenge his assumptions.

'I… I don't understand. Why would you want to be
here, of all places? It's about as far from your homeland
as you could possibly get…'

She sighed again, and Lucius got the feeling that
she didn't really know the answer to that question
herself. They heard Quin murmur softly in his sleep
and were quiet for a while.

When Isi spoke again, a wistful tone had entered
her voice: 'I used to think of Egypt as home, it's true.
That was until I went there and realised I didn't belong.
Now, I don't know where my home is. Perhaps I don't
have one… I was happy enough travelling around
with the Swords of Isis. But I'm also happy being here
with you and Quin, exploring this strange world of the
far north.'

'That's good to hear,' said Lucius, 'because
sometimes I get the feeling you wish you hadn't come.'

'If I didn't want to be here, I'd leave,' she said simply.
'I came here to help you with your quest, Lucius. Did
you think I would abandon you?'

* *Mare Nostrum: 'our sea', a Roman name for the Mediterranean Sea.*

He felt heartened by these words, but also a little troubled by them. There was something cold about the way she spoke, as though describing a duty she had set herself. There was no mention of friendship. Had he killed something between them when he'd supported Eprius against her? A sense of trust, perhaps? He remembered how they used to laugh together back at Gladiator School, and the sheer joy of their reunion the night she rescued him in Carthage. He wished he could get that feeling back again somehow.

Eventually he fell asleep, and dreamed of marching down an endless road – left, right, left, right, left…

CHAPTER V

21–26 MAY

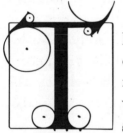he next day, after breakfast, they continued with their training. More marching – Gallicus was obsessed with it! They spent the entire morning going up and down the Via Principalis – this time in full armour. Lucius could feel the blisters forming on the soles of his feet, and his arms and legs ached from having to keep them so straight and raise them so high – but as the hours passed, he started to discover a certain rhythm, and the air vibrated slightly less frequently with the bellows and curses of the big centurion.

In the afternoon, to their relief, they finally moved on to weapons training. For this session they were joined by five other recent recruits. Gallicus could only look on, his jaw slack with astonishment, as Lucius, Isi and Quin showed off their swordfighting skills on the wooden posts. Moving like the fearsome Spartoi[*] of Greek legend, they displayed the full repertoire of cuts, thrusts, stabs, feints and lunges. They managed this despite using wooden swords and shields weighted with iron to make them even heavier than their standard weaponry. Perhaps because the trio had surprised him with their talents, Gallicus seemed to take a sadistic relish in pushing them harder and for longer than the other recruits. Long after their fellow munifices[**] had retired to the bathhouse, he forced them on. By the time he finally let them rest, Lucius's arms were crying out their pain.

That evening, at dinner, he could barely raise his soup spoon to his lips. 'I... am... dead,' he groaned.

'I hate Gallicus,' Isi muttered to herself, as she massaged her sword arm. 'I curse him. Petbe,[***] Lord of the Sky, please make that man suffer.'

Even Quin was looking drained, but he managed a thin smile. 'Can you imagine how easy it'll be to fight with our real weapons now we've got used to these heavier ones?' he said.

'Why did he make us work so much harder than the others?' complained Lucius.

'He obviously saw our potential,' said Quin. 'He's

* *Spartoi: fierce warriors who grew from dragon's teeth.*

** *munifices: ordinary soldiers, privates.*

*** *Petbe: the Egyptian god of revenge.*

grooming us for a quick promotion. You just wait – in a few weeks we'll be immunes.'*

The next few days were a mixture of mind-numbing tedium, mind-aching exertion and, in Lucius's case, frequent humiliation. Mornings were spent marching, now with full armour, weapons and kit. They were taught the various army drills and formations – how to move as if part of a 'single, deadly animal', as Gallicus described it. They learned their place in formation, and they memorised the shouted commands and trumpet blasts that were the signals to change from a single line into a square or a wedge, a defensive circle or a testudo.** They were instructed how to fall back through lines of relieving troops without disrupting them, and what to do if a line was broken by the enemy – all while moving forwards, backwards or sideways at high speed. While Quin and Isi were quick to learn the drills, Lucius and another recruit, Juvenius, struggled and were often singled out for a bawling from Gallicus.

Drills were followed by sessions on the vaulting horse in the barracks. At Gallicus's command, they were expected to leap on or over the wooden horse in full armour and weapons. The ill-fitting armour chafed

* *immunes: soldiers with special responsibilities.*

** *testudo: Latin for 'tortoise' – a formation in which a group of soldiers packed themselves tightly together and overlapped their shields for protection.*

Lucius painfully as he leapt, and his skin after these sessions was always covered in purple bruises. Every time he slipped and fell – which seemed to happen to him a lot more than to anyone else – Gallicus would roar in his ear: 'You stupid clot! What if that happens in battle, eh? What if you lose your footing while you're climbing a scaling ladder or leaping a rampart? You'll be condemning all those behind you to death! Now see you don't do it again!'

Afternoons were devoted to weapons training, either with the gladius or with the spear, or pilum. Here, at last, was something Lucius could excel at. With his experience as a Hoplomachus, he easily outshone all the other recruits with the pilum. He could jab and thrust with it like a veteran, and hurl it accurately enough to strike a man-sized wooden post at thirty paces. Gallicus paired up the recruits so they could practise hand-to-hand combat with pila and shields. Even though the steel tips of the pila had been covered by leather pads, the jabs could still be painful.

On the fourth day of training, Gallicus himself decided to spar with Lucius. The instructor came at Lucius hard, but he sidestepped, deflecting the power of the blow with his shield. The bigger man snarled and came at him again. Lucius parried. He fought within himself, sensing he had the measure of the man, but not wishing to humiliate him for fear of incurring his wrath. So he backstepped and deflected, ducked and blocked, trying to avoid injury while shying away from anything offensive. He could see Gallicus's blood starting to boil at these defensive tactics – but what else could he do? It was almost as if Gallicus *wanted* to hurt him. He wondered what he could have done to offend him.

Eventually, Gallicus tired of trying to break through Lucius's stubborn defences and resorted to goading him. He circled him and prodded him with his spear as if he were a wild beast. 'C'mon, gladiator boy! Show us what you're made of!' Lucius slowly turned so he was always facing the instructor, calmly deflecting the prods but not counterattacking. He saw that Gallicus was sweating and breathing heavily. Was that fear behind his smile of bravado? The man was big but quite slow, and Lucius felt certain he could take him. Three swift movements was all it would take: pilum, shield, then pilum. He could strike like lightning and the centurion would be on the ground before he knew what had hit him.

A quietness had descended on the training ground. Lucius became aware that the other pairs had stopped fighting and had gathered in a circle to watch him square off against the instructor whom many of them had come to loathe. Some of the recruits seemed to be silently urging him to attack. This was hardly surprising – of course, they'd love to see Gallicus take a beating, especially as they wouldn't have to face the consequences. And what would those consequences be? He'd heard rumours of brutal army punishments

– deprivation of rations, flogging, even being kicked to death. Who could say what Gallicus would do after being humiliated in front of his protégés?

Lucius caught sight of Quin restlessly grinding his teeth and squeezing the shaft of his spear. He was glaring enviously at his brother, wishing he could be fighting Gallicus instead. *I wish it, too, Brother*, thought Lucius. Somehow, he sensed, Quin would have found a dignified way out of this, avoiding a mauling while allowing Gallicus to save face. Isi was also watching Lucius, discreetly shaking her head at him. She knew how much he longed to wipe the smile off Gallicus's face – and how bad it would be for him if he did. But the instructor was steadily pushing him beyond the point of reason. 'You're not a gladiator, are you?' he cried. 'You're a little girl! You don't belong here, little girl. Why don't you go back to mummy?'

Of course Gallicus had his own supporters among the recruits – the sycophantic types found in every unit who automatically side with those in power, hoping it will further them in their careers. They were making themselves heard now, laughing with glee at every mocking comment from their hero.

Gallicus stung Lucius with a sharp prod to his unguarded shoulder. 'Come on, you coward,' he spat. 'I'll bet your father was no better. A coward too, was he?'

Lucius acted then. Of course Gallicus couldn't have known the truth about his father, but just hearing him say those words was like a crack of the whip. Lucius struck without thinking, without even planning to do so – almost as if his body had taken the decision without waiting for his mind to agree. And that was probably what saved him, because Gallicus had been watching his opponent's face for mood shifts – the best clue to any fighter's intentions – ready to spring a counterattack. But Lucius's face had been blank when he began his attack, and by the time his expression had twisted itself into a scowl of rage, he was already halfway through the first of his three strikes – rotating his shoulders anticlockwise to land a blow to Gallicus's right flank. Gallicus could only parry with his shield, opening himself to a frontal attack from Lucius, who struck the big man forcefully beneath the chin with the upper edge of his shield. As Gallicus rocked backwards, it was an easy task to ram the pilum's tip hard into his breastplate, sending him crashing to the ground.

Silence.

Gallicus's supporters looked as though they had been struck themselves. No one, apart from Isi and Quin, had ever witnessed such a devastating display up close. This was what gladiator school gave its alumni – swiftness in the attack, and a shattering, traumatising power in the strike.

Gallicus didn't move at first. He was dazed, but not unconscious. He reached up and rubbed the reddening mark on his chin. His eyes, as they lost their glazed look, deepened to the colour of the stormclouds Lucius had often seen gathering above the Caledonian mountains. Any sense of satisfaction was fleeting, quickly replaced with foreboding.

Someone in the crowd of recruits foolishly began to laugh. His laughter echoed around the walls of the courtyard like the braying and snorting of a donkey. Lucius looked up and saw that it was Juvenius. *Shut up, you idiot!* he wanted to shout. *You're going to make things worse.*

The laughter roused Gallicus. He sat up, still rubbing his chin. The laughter died as he scanned the line of recruits. 'Who laughed?' he asked. These were the quietest words he'd ever uttered, and they sent cool ripples of fear down every spine in the grounds. 'Who laughed?' he asked again, his tone almost friendly.

Eventually, the guilty one stepped forward.

'This amuses you, does it, Juvenius?' said Gallicus, still sounding quite amiable.

'N-no, sir.'

Gallicus rose to his feet and drew closer to the unfortunate soldier. 'Oh, so why did you laugh, then?'

'Don't know, sir.'

'Perhaps you're looking for something amusing, something to laugh at. Of course, that must be it!' He sneered. 'Tell you what, why don't you go extra muros tonight, Juvenius? Would that be amusing enough for you, hmm?'

Juvenius's face turned white as Parian marble. His

jaw flapped as he tried to form words but couldn't. 'N-n-n-no… P-p-p-p-please, sir…'

Extra muros meant sleeping outside the walls of the camp. Such was the paranoia enveloping Pinnata these days, Lucius had discovered, that no one – not even the hunting and foraging parties – ventured out these days without an armed escort. That was why the recruits were doing all their training inside the camp. Sending a single legionary to spend a night outside the walls on his own seemed tantamount to murder.

Lucius briefly wondered if he would be sent to join Juvenius, but it quickly became clear that he wouldn't. In fact, incredibly, he appeared to have evaded punishment altogether. Gallicus left the training ground soon after passing sentence on Juvenius, without even a parting glance at the boy who'd bested him. Lucius looked on pityingly as Juvenius was led away by guards. The young recruit's foolishness had probably saved Lucius's skin by allowing Gallicus to find another, more convenient target for his frustration. Juvenius was still shaking his head and muttering to himself as he departed, seemingly unable to take in what was happening to him.

That night, Juvenius pitched his tent as close as he could to the outer ramparts of the fort. The following morning he was gone, along with his tent and all his kit. Soldiers searching the site could find no sign of his presence, except for a small area of flattened grass. The night guards who'd been on duty swore they'd neither seen nor heard anything. Assuming he hadn't completely lost his wits and gone wandering off on his own, the only possible conclusion was that he had been spirited away by the enemy. The camp prefect* ordered a search of the immediate vicinity, but no evidence of poor Juvenius was discovered. The story of the hapless soldier spread quickly around the camp as only bad news can, adding to the myth that their enemy possessed almost supernatural powers.

Over breakfast, Cornix gave everyone his version of what must have happened. 'The Caledonians must have stolen in and slit the boy's throat before he could cry out,' he said while chewing on his bacon. 'Then they carried him and his possessions away.'

'They did all that within twenty paces of the nearest watchtower?' said Quin incredulously.

'They did,' nodded Cornix. 'And there's only one thing can explain it…' His voice dropped to a whisper. 'Those Caledonians ain't human. They're demons. They can blend into the trees, make themselves invisible, like the wind – and before you know it… they've got you!'

An uneasy silence fell around the table. Then Cornix cackled with mirth, breaking the tension. 'That's got you worried, hasn't it?' he chuckled, before continuing

* *camp prefect: third-in-command of a Roman legion.*

more seriously: "Course I don't hold with any of that supernatural talk. But if you ask me, the Caledonians are definitely up to something. This Juvenius business is just the beginning. Don't forget, Agricola's stripped Pinnata of half its men to go off on his fort-building exercise. He's left us practically defenceless – and the enemy know it…'

Lucius found it hard to concentrate on training that day. He kept thinking about poor Juvenius, and couldn't help feeling a little bit responsible for the boy's fate. He also missed the boy's presence – his clumsiness, his perpetual good cheer and his invincible enthusiasm. Juvenius hadn't meant to laugh at Gallicus – Lucius was sure of that. He'd just found the situation funny, and couldn't help himself. Now he was dead, most likely. Gallicus, of course, didn't mention the incident, and affected not to notice the sombre mood of the recruits.

Despite his uneasy state of mind, sleep came swiftly for Lucius that night, as it always did after an exhausting day of training. At some unknown hour, he was woken by shouting outside their barrack room. He smelled smoke in the air and heard the whinnying of horses and the screaming of soldiers outside. Even then, he failed at first to rise, so thick was the fug of sleep in his brain.

'What's going on?' he heard Quin groan.

Forcing his eyes open, Lucius saw that Isi was already standing at the barred window of their dormitory. 'Gods!' she whispered. 'No!'

That did it. The boys leapt out of bed and ran to join her at the window. When Lucius saw the view outside, he wondered for a moment if he was still asleep, racked by some terrible dream. The night was ablaze. Many of the camp's wooden buildings were on fire, and silhouetted against the flames were visions of utter horror: tall, hairy figures were running through the smoke and sparks, yelling their war cries and swinging their heavy iron battleaxes. Tunic-clad soldiers were streaming out of their burning barrack blocks only to be hacked down by the axes as they emerged. In the orange half-light Lucius witnessed limbs and heads being severed from bodies in single blows. The Via Principalis was awash with blood. It was a massacre.

Quin was already strapping on his cuirass and picking up his sword. 'Come on! We have to get out there and fight them.'

Lucius was transfixed like a rabbit in the glow of a hunter's lamp. The sight of the maimed and slaughtered, and those giant swinging axes gleaming with fresh blood, froze him with fear. He knew they'd be cut down as soon as they stepped out.

'We're on fire,' he heard Isi cry. She pointed out of the window at the roof of their barrack block. Already, thick, choking waves of smoke were gusting into their dormitory. Their world had suddenly narrowed to two stark choices: stay here and burn, or go out there and fight the axemen.

Lucius and Isi began donning their armour.

Outside, the camp's defenders had begun to mount a resistance to the invaders. A column of armoured troops charged in along the Via Decumana* from the farther side of the camp. They didn't look too numerous, and Lucius was reminded of Cornix's warning about Agricola leaving the fort undermanned. The troops launched their spears towards the Caledonians. A few were felled, but unfortunately, in all the smoke and confusion, some of the spears also impaled fellow Romans who were fleeing the scene.

As the Caledonians rounded on the Roman column, Quin charged out, trailed by Isi and finally Lucius, a loose sandal strap still flapping. Isi had tucked her mother's mirror into her belt before leaving. Seeing this reminded Lucius of his own precious possessions: he dashed back into the dormitory and retrieved his father's ring and tiny wooden dog from his kit. By the time he re-emerged from the building, he saw that half a dozen other soldiers had joined them on their side of the Via Principalis. Together they launched themselves at the Caledonians, who were surprised by an attack to their rear. Lucius caught sight of Quin to his left, swinging his sword at one of them and knocking him

---

* *Via Decumana (or Decumanus Maximus): the main east–west street in a Roman camp.*

off his feet, before dispatching him with a thrust of his blade into the throat. To his right, Isi was engaged in a fierce fight against another hairy invader – axe against sword.

An axe blade whispered through the air. Lucius jerked himself backwards as gleaming death brushed by, close enough to nick the skin on his cheek. He swung his sword and felt the thud of sharpened metal cutting into flesh and bone. Blood splashed his face. In less than a second, it was over. A man he had never known lay dead at his feet. Before he had time to reflect on this, more Caledonians appeared out of the smoke. Lucius took a firmer grip on his sword and charged at the first one. He fought as he had been trained: punch with the shield boss, thrust upwards into the stomach with the sword, then twist and pull to extract it. Punch, thrust, twist and pull. The man toppled even before he could raise his axe. Another one loomed, this one carrying a spear. Lucius deflected the spear with his sword, then punched at the enemy's face with his shield. His sword ended the man's life before he even hit the ground.

After a week of solid training, formation had become almost second nature to Lucius, Quin and Isi, and even in the mêlée of battle, they managed to hold their line, always keeping abreast of each other. This was fortunate because the next attack came from Lucius's unshielded side. A Caledonian swordsman swung his sword hard and low from the right. Isi, seeing this, managed to raise her own shield in time to divert a strike that could have severed Lucius's leg.

Still the Caledonians came. There seemed no end to them. Lucius, Quin and Isi found themselves being slowly driven back towards the burning barracks from where they'd escaped. They saw their fellow Romans dying beside them, but the trio held firm, their gladiator skills, together with their legionary discipline, keeping them alive. Punch, thrust, twist, pull... Punch, thrust, twist, pull... They were locked in the legionary's dance of death, as bodies began to pile up by their feet. Lucius kept hoping that the Caledonians' will would eventually break and they'd turn and flee – but they didn't, and new ones kept on arriving to take the places of their dead comrades. Cornix's words flashed into Lucius's mind: 'When they come, it'll be like the sea. They'll sweep us right out of Caledonia.' The three of them were being driven back very close to the inferno that had been their barracks. Lucius could feel the fierce heat against his back, and he was almost choked by the stink of blood and smoke. His shoulders ached, and his arm felt like lead. His blade was losing its edge after all the bone it had been driven into. His hands were now slippery with blood, and more than once he almost lost his grip on his sword during the twist and pull.

There came a cry to his left, and he saw Quin go down amid a mass of red-haired warriors. The pressure they were under had driven the brothers apart, and now Quin was too far away to be rescued. One of the Caledonians drove his sword downwards at Quin's prone figure. Lucius barged in with his shield, but knew he would not make it in time. At the very last moment, with the sword tip just inches from Quin's heaving stomach, a hand jetted out from the horde of warriors and clasped the swordsman's wrist, stopping his blade in mid-plunge.

The swordsman was thrust aside as another man – the one who'd just stopped him – pushed his way forward and bent closer to Quin. The Caledonians around him stopped fighting and stared at their comrade. Even Lucius and Isi ceased combat, incredulous at what they were seeing. Like all the Caledonians, Quin's rescuer wore his hair long, but his hair was dark, and his beard was forked into two plaited strands. The clasps of his belt and cloak gleamed with gold, marking him out as a noble or a chieftain. The Caledonian knelt beside Quin and examined the pendant around his neck – the one of black stone, silver and enamel that Quin had taken from the man he'd killed up on the ridge. Then the Caledonian looked up and said something to those near him. One of them immediately grabbed Quin's wrists, the other his ankles, and together they raised him from the ground. Quin struggled, but was helpless against their strength.

On the far side of the street, the battle between the Caledonians and the Romans continued, but here the fight was over: with Quin captured, Lucius and Isi were the only remaining defenders still on their feet. As the two warriors began carrying Quin away, Lucius raised his sword and charged at them, prepared to die to save his brother. But before he could reach them, he felt himself being lifted off the ground and raised high in the air. The stars above him wheeled dizzily as he was swung around as if made of straw. He felt himself in the grip of something huge and monstrous, like a sailor of Odysseus about to be devoured by a cyclops.*

Quin's voice cried out somewhere below him, and then he heard the Caledonian with the forked beard bark another order. To Lucius, it sounded like 'Leeg as, Baltair!' He felt himself falling. His armoured shoulder clanged against stone, sending a shock of pain through his upper body. He looked up and saw, against the smoky-orange horizon, the giant who had lifted him so effortlessly. Fierce dark eyes simmered beneath a great ridge of brow. From the stone-grey slabs of his cheeks down through the massive arch of his shoulders to the boulder-sized muscles that jutted from his bare arms and chest, he appeared like some natural formation, a rocky outcrop of the hills.

The next thing Lucius knew, the giant hoisted him up once again and slung him over his shoulders, then began carrying him down the Via Principalis

---

* *cyclops: a one-eyed giant of ancient Greek legend. In the* Odyssey *(the great Greek epic by Homer), the cyclops Polyphemus kills and eats several of Odysseus's men.*

like a shepherd with a lamb. Lucius was vaguely aware of Quin somewhere below him, jouncing along between two Caledonians, and Isi, similarly helpless, being carried along on the other side. This couldn't be happening! Lucius couldn't bear the thought of being enslaved by these people, to be tortured or mistreated at their pleasure. He'd sooner die fighting them. Exhausted though he was, he wrestled against the grip of his captor with every ounce of energy he still possessed, pulling, kicking, scratching and biting. The giant cursed him and dug his nails hard into the skin of his leg, but Lucius refused to stop. Eventually he managed to pull his arm free of the giant's fist and began pummelling his stomach. The warrior emitted an irritated grunt and removed a small hammer from his belt. He swept his arm upwards – and then everything went dark.

CHAPTER VI

26 MAY

ucius awoke with a terrible headache and with the taste of blood in his mouth. When he opened his eyes, the scene was too blurry to make anything out, but it was bright enough to make him blink. He could smell manure and cooking meat, and hear blacksmiths' hammers, chickens clucking and, in the background, a soft wailing.

Gradually, the shapes around him became clearer. He was lying on hard, dry earth beneath an open sky. He was wearing his tunic – his armour and weapons were gone. His arms and legs were almost black with soot and blood. Wanting to rid himself of the horrible taste, he tried to spit, but his mouth was too dry and he could only produce a sticky stream of pink drool that stuck to his tunic. He rubbed his head, trying to block out the pain. He longed for a drink of water.

Sitting a few yards away were Quin and Isi, looking similarly filthy, but otherwise OK. He sighed with relief. The three of them were in an enclosure of about six paces in diameter, surrounded by a dense timber latticework wall. It was like a cage, but open at the top. The walls could be climbed easily enough, but the row of pointed wooden stakes that topped them were tall and sharp enough to deter any thoughts of escape. Two wooden doors, placed opposite each other, gave access to the cage. Quin and Isi were seated near one of these doors, leaning back against the wall, their eyes closed. Flinching from the pain that flared in his head as he moved, Lucius struggled over to join them.

'What's going on?' he croaked.

'You're awake!' said Isi, opening her eyes and smiling at him. 'How are you feeling?'

'I've been better,' said Lucius, tenderly feeling the bump on his head. 'Where are we?'

'In a hilltop village somewhere to the northwest of Pinnata, as far as we can make out,' said Quin.

Lucius peered between the square spaces in the latticework and saw that they were, indeed, located on the edge of a busy village. The entire settlement, including their cage, was surrounded by a palisade of sharpened stakes. Guards with shields and spears patrolled a platform that ran around the inside of the palisade. The village contained simple structures of wood and animal hide, as well as larger dwellings with low, circular stone walls topped by conical grass roofs. Seated in front of these were men and women busy with their work – spinning, weaving, hammering hot metal, and woodturning on pole lathes. Smoke rose out of the earth from underground ovens. Chickens clucked and squawked and children ran around laughing. Most of the people had red hair, though a few were dark. They wore colourful tunics, leggings and cloaks.

'Isn't it wonderful!' said Isi, following his gaze. 'These people have probably lived like this for hundreds, maybe thousands of years, in perfect harmony with nature. What possible need have they of Roman civilisation?' She said the last word with a sneer in her voice.

Lucius observed the excitement in her eyes as she took in the scene. He couldn't think how to respond. It was true – right now, Rome did seem a long way away. Its great temples and statues, its aqueducts and bathhouses, of which Romans were so proud, would look quite alien in this landscape. Why were the legions even here? What did they hope to bring to these people?'

The wailing sound he'd heard earlier started up again. It was, he now understood, the weeping of women, seated alone in front of their dwellings. They were crying, he guessed, for the men who hadn't come back last night. Some of those men he'd probably killed himself. It suddenly hit him that these people were prepared to sacrifice everything, even the lives of their loved ones, to keep their freedom.

'I'm surprised we're still alive,' he muttered.

'I was thinking the same thing,' said Quin, who was trying to wipe some of the soot off his face with the sleeve of his tunic. 'We killed so many of them. Why spare us, and no one else?'

Then a memory came back to Lucius. 'One of them caught sight of your pendant,' he said. 'I think that was when they decided not to kill us.'

'You're right,' said Quin. He felt around his neck, but the only thing hanging there now was his signaculum. 'That fellow must have swiped it. I wonder what it meant to him.'

A young male Caledonian approached their cage and peered in. 'Lucius?' he said. 'Is that you underneath all that soot?'

Lucius stared at the boy, stunned to be identified by one of the barbarians – and also to hear him speak in Latin. Then he realised who he was looking at. He hadn't recognised him at first in his Caledonian-style cloak and leggings. Despite the pain he was in, Lucius managed to clamber to his feet. He pushed his hand through the woven wall and clasped the boy's wrist.

'Juvenius! You're alive!'

Juvenius hastily removed his hand and glanced nervously over his shoulder. 'I shouldn't be talking to you,' he said, 'but I'm glad you survived.' He squinted at the other two for a moment. 'You, also, Quintus and Amulius.'

'Why did they keep you alive?' asked Quin.

Juvenius looked down, ashamed. 'They used me,' he said. 'I'm sorry, but I helped them break into Pinnata last night.'

'What?' snapped Quin, leaping to his feet and gripping the cage wall.

The boy checked over his shoulder once again to make sure no one was looking his way. Then he explained in a hurried whisper: 'They forced me to go back there. I had to go up to the gate and beg the guards to let me enter. The guards were so surprised and happy to see me, they forgot the drill. It never crossed their minds it might be a trap. As soon as they opened the gates, the Caledonians, who'd been waiting in the trees just beyond the ramparts, charged...'

Hearing this, Quin reached through the wall and grabbed Juvenius by the scruff of his tunic, pulling him hard towards him so his cheek was pressed tightly against one of the vertical stakes.

'Traitor!' Quin hissed.

'I had no choice,' whined Juvenius. 'They were going to kill me.'

'You should have let them,' growled Quin. 'Do you know how many of your comrades died last night?'

'Leave him, Quin!' warned Isi.

There was a movement to their left and a sword tip jabbed against Quin's neck. Lucius spun around and saw that three Caledonian men had stealthily entered the cage from the door on the far side. The closest of them held the sword that was now threatening Quin's jugular He was the giant who had picked Lucius up last night. He looked no less fierce in daylight.

Calmly, Quin flicked away Juvenius and turned, so the sword was now pointing towards his throat. He raised his hands in submission, as Juvenius scurried away.

Lucius read rage and hatred in the giant's face. 'You Romans!' he spat, looking at each of them in turn. 'You kill many of my brothers. All good, brave men. You die for this, I hope. Chief Calgacus say today you must live. But I pray to the great goddess Cailleach that tomorrow the chief change his mind, so I can kill you.'

Quin, to his credit, did not look intimidated by the giant's muscles or his words. 'That's why he's chief and you're not,' he said with a nonchalant smile. 'He's got brains.' Quin tapped his head with his finger. 'Calgacus knows that if he kills us, our chief Agricola will come here and burn your village to the ground.'

The giant's fist kneaded his sword handle ferociously. His eyes seethed with the desire to kill. Lucius prayed Quin wouldn't goad him any further. 'I am Baltair,' said the giant. 'I fear no man. I swear to you now I will kill you – all of you. And when Agricola comes, I will kill him also.'

Then, with a swirl of his cloak, he departed with his two accomplices.

'Be careful, Quin,' said Lucius, when they were

alone again. 'That man looked very close to losing it.'

'Him?' said Quin carelessly. 'He doesn't scare me.'

'You've never faced an enemy that size before.'

'The bigger they are, the harder they fall,' was Quin's muttered response.

'Chief Calgacus,' said Isi thoughtfully. 'Didn't Cornix mention him? He's the one who's supposed to be uniting all the tribes of Caledonia. Do you think he was the man with the double beard.'

'I'd say so,' said Lucius. 'He looked like their leader.'

This captured Quin's attention. 'Just think,' he said, '– if we could kill him, that would break the Caledonian resistance once and for all.'

'There's gratitude for you!' said Isi sharply. 'Don't forget, it was Calgacus who saved our lives last night – and from what Baltair was saying, he's the only one keeping us alive right now.'

'All the same, I –' Quin stopped in mid-sentence, distracted by something he'd seen in the village. 'Hey-ho!' he smiled. 'Look what's coming our way.'

The other two looked, and saw a village girl approaching the cage, laden with a bucket of water.

'Water!' cried Lucius.

'And food!' laughed Isi, spying the loaf of bread tucked under the girl's arm.

But Quin's attention was on neither of these – only on the person conveying them.

The girl entered the cage like a skittish young deer. Keeping her eyes close to the ground, she placed the bucket of water and the bread before them, then reached into her cloak and drew out a leg of lamb, which she laid next to the bread. Lucius immediately took up the ladle in the bucket and began pouring water down his parched throat. It felt so good to wash away the dry, salty taste of blood. He gargled and swilled it around happily. Even his headache started to subside. Then he handed the ladle on to Isi before tearing off a chunk of bread. The bread was freshly baked, and tasted and smelled delicious. It was only once he was chomping gleefully on this that he noticed the staring thing going on between Quin and the Caledonian girl. She was half-turned away from them, as if in the act of leaving – but seemed as strangely transfixed by the sight of Quin as he was by her.

Lucius flicked his head from one to the other, first in curiosity and then in rising alarm. *Please*, he begged Cupid, who was the god in charge of such matters, *please don't let Quin fall for a Caledonian girl! We're in enough trouble as it is!*

But it appeared that Cupid's arrow had already struck – and in both directions. Not even the food and water could tempt Quin right now. And as for the girl, she appeared rooted to the spot, as if she had forgotten where she was and what she had come here for. She was, Lucius supposed, beautiful in the Caledonian style – with soft, pale skin, big green eyes, long red hair and a dainty pink mouth. He could see why Quin could take a fancy to such a creature – but had he completely forgotten that she was the enemy?

Quin rose catlike to his feet and began circling her – keeping his eyes fixed on her all the while, as hers were on him – until he was facing her. He moved slightly towards her, and she nervously backed off. He put his hand to his chest. 'I… am… Quintus,' he said gently. Then he pointed at her. 'You… are?'

She didn't reply at first. Then, in a hesitant voice, she said 'Flo-ree' – and ran away.

Quin started after her, but Isi grabbed his arm. 'Bad idea, Quin,' she said.

The girl had left the cage door swinging open. Within a minute, she had returned, this time clutching a small yellow flower, freshly plucked. She held up the flower and, again, said 'Flo-ree', then pointed to herself and once again repeated the word.

Quin looked puzzled. 'Is she saying she's a flower?' he said, turning to Lucius.

'No,' said Lucius. 'She's saying her name means "flower".'

Quin turned back to the girl. 'Pleased to meet you, Floree,' he said solemnly.

She handed him the flower. He took it, letting his fingers linger on hers. Then he raised it to his nostrils and breathed in its scent. He took her hand and kissed it.

Floree blushed. She pulled her hand free and ran at full speed from the cage. Clumsy in her haste, she shut and bolted the gate before hurrying away. It was only when she was safely back in the village that she dared look back. Quin waved to her from behind the cage wall. She stared back at him for a moment, before disappearing inside one of the round houses with cone-shaped roofs.

Quin laughed in delight and sniffed the flower. 'Floree,' he grinned. 'Isn't she lovely?'

'You're crazy,' said Lucius.

'You're a fool,' said Isi.

'I'm in love,' said Quin.

That afternoon, while Quin was in the middle of torturing Lucius and Isi with his atrocious poetry ('Floree – eyes as green as a Caledonian vallee…'), they received a visit from four powerful-looking Caledonian men with spears. Lucius was relieved that none of them was Baltair. Yet he was filled with foreboding. Was this it? Had Baltair won the argument against Calgacus? Were they about to be executed? Silently, the Caledonians motioned the prisoners to follow them. Two of the guards walked ahead, and the other two brought up the rear, as they escorted the prisoners out of the cage and along the path that led to the village.

Lucius felt the heat of the villagers' stares as they walked among them. He kept his head up and back straight, wanting to show these people that, even if he was their prisoner, he was still a Roman and proud of it. He was pleased he and the other two had managed to clean themselves up a bit – washing themselves in what remained of the water after they'd drunk their fill.

Quin, he noticed, was scanning the faces of the villagers, no doubt hoping for a sight of Floree. When he saw her, a grin lit up his face. She was standing among the watching crowd, holding hands with a boy of six or seven, perhaps her brother. Quin blew her a kiss. She blushed and turned away, but couldn't prevent a smile sneaking onto her face. Seeing this, Lucius quietly cursed Cupid. Quin would have noticed the smile too, which would only encourage him in his stupid passion, putting them in even more danger. Lucius also saw Juvenius among the crowd, still wearing the native garb that looked so ridiculous on him. Did the boy have no pride? How quickly he'd surrendered his Romanness and taken on the appearance of a barbarian. When Juvenius waved at him, Lucius turned away in disgust.

They were led into the largest structure of the settlement: a round house near the centre of the village that stood almost twice the height of the others. Passing through an animal-hide curtain, they entered the interior. The smoky air was, at first, hard to breathe. Through watery eyes, Lucius took in his surroundings. Smoke rose from a dying fire on the central hearth, up into the timber-framed conical roof space before disappearing through a hole at the top. The hearth was surrounded by a circle of logs, which served as benches for the men seated in the room. Spears, swords and oval shields lined the stone walls, lending the room a military atmosphere – not homely at all.

Lucius recognised the giant Baltair among the seated men, as well as the fork-bearded man they'd seen the night before, who he assumed was Calgacus. Four other men sat with them, all powerful, solemn-faced men of middle years or older. They wore their hair long with plaited strands, and long, drooping moustaches. Their colourful patchwork cloaks were pinned to their shoulders with finely worked brooches, and they wore golden torcs* around their necks. Each man had at least two armed bodyguards standing close behind him.

Forkbeard and several others raised their heads as the prisoners entered. Baltair didn't – he just stared at the hearth, the fury that boiled in his eyes looking intense enough to relight it. Forkbeard, Lucius noted, was holding Quin's pendant in his hand, running his thumb over its black, green and silver surface.

'Welcome, Romans,' said Forkbeard. His voice was soft, yet full of authority – a voice that did not exactly command obedience, yet somehow expected it. 'I am Calgacus, chief of the Damnonii. You have already met my right-hand man Baltair. May I introduce Torcall of

* torcs: metal neck-rings, usually made from strands of bronze or gold twisted together.

the Taexali, Raghnall of the Selgovae, Morven of the Otadini and Asgall of the Novantae.' The men nodded their heads as Calgacus gestured to each of them in turn. 'I know you Romans like to think of us as one people – you call us Caledonians to make things simpler for yourselves – but there are many tribes in the north, and the men you see gathered here are the chiefs of the most powerful of those tribes. Yet it appears that you may have got what you wanted, because we have agreed to form a confederation of tribes, under my leadership, to win back the land you have stolen from us. You wanted one enemy. Well, now you have it. Our attack on your fort last night was the first taste of what is to come.'

Baltair spat into the hearth. He gabbled angrily to Calgacus in their own tongue, until Calgacus put up his hand and the giant fell into a surly silence.

'Baltair wants to know why I waste my time talking to you young Romans. He wants to know why I don't just kill you now.' He paused, contemplating once again the pendant in his hand. A weariness seemed to descend upon his shoulders, making him appear older. 'This belonged to my father,' he said, holding up the pendant. 'He was a great warrior, and he made the Damnonii powerful. But he was killed during a battle with our most hated enemies, the Venicones. The one who killed him stole this amulet from his body. If I am grateful to you Romans for anything, it is for the destruction of the Venicones.' He looked at Quin. 'You fought against them, did you?' he asked.

Quin shook his head.

'Then how did you come by this?' He held up the pendant.

'Some people ambushed us in the hills,' said Quin. 'We killed them. One of them was wearing it.'

'You are a fine warrior,' he said, nodding. 'I saw that much last night. I spared you and your two friends because when I saw this around your neck, I knew that you must have slain my father's killer. And it seems you did. One good turn deserves another, yes?'

'Thank you,' said Quin. 'So what do you plan to do with us?'

Calgacus stood up. He moved closer to the prisoners, his lively, intelligent eyes playing over their eyes and faces as if trying to access their thoughts. 'I will answer that shortly,' he said. 'But first, I have a question for you: why are you here?'

'You captured us,' said Quin.

Calgacus showed no irritation at this deliberate misunderstanding of his question. He merely clarified: 'I mean here in the north. Why do you Romans need this land? Do you not have enough already?'

Lucius cleared his throat. 'We want to share with you the benefits of our civilisation,' he said. 'We want you to live in comfort, as we do, as citizens of our empire. Your history is one of bloodshed and war. Before the Romans came, you fought against each other, tribe against tribe. We want to offer you peace.'

Calgacus nodded, stroking his beard. 'Civilisation… peace… and how would you like us to repay you for these wonderful gifts?'

There were smiles on the faces of the men around the hearth, and Lucius sensed that the chieftain was playing with him.

'By… by paying taxes,' he said.

'By paying taxes,' repeated Calgacus mildly. Then, slowly, his face changed. A flush appeared high in his cheeks and powerful muscles tensed in his jaws. 'You robbers!' he suddenly bellowed. 'You bandits! You have plundered our lands, destroyed our crops, slaughtered our women and children, and you call it civilisation! You create devastation and you call it peace! And after all that, you dare to demand… taxes?'

'We don't want to fight you,' pleaded Lucius. 'If you… if you could only see how we live – how you could live, too, if you chose to. If you would only accept us, we could build you cities linked by networks of roads. We could pipe fresh water straight from the mountains into those cities until their fountains overflowed. We could heat your homes and build you bathhouses where you could bathe in heated water. We could build fine temples to your gods, and provide teachers for your children and doctors for when you get sick, and… and so much more. I can't begin to describe to you all the wonders we could give you…'

Lucius trailed away when he saw the lack of reaction on the faces of those he'd been hoping to persuade.

Calgacus was calm again in his reply: 'You can keep your cities and your roads, young man. You can keep your hot baths. And we are content to sacrifice to our gods in groves, rivers and bogs as we have always done. Thank you for the offer, but really, we're fine! All we want is to be left alone, to be able to live as we've always lived… But to do that – to get back to how things were before your people came and turned our lives upside down – we'll need some help… from you.'

'I don't understand,' said Lucius.

Calgacus went over to the wall and unhooked a long iron sword. He held the heavy weapon in both hands, brandishing it expertly. 'You Romans know how to fight,' he said. 'Although we could probably beat any one of you man-to-man, as a unit, in the field, you're unstoppable. You move together, almost like… like a single creature…' He danced around in the space beside the hearth, the sword flashing in the light cast by the dying embers. The chieftain swung the weapon with a blend of fluid grace and deadly precision that Lucius could not help but admire. After a while, Calgacus laid the sword down by the hearth, and his attention wandered back to the pendant, which was now dangling around his neck. He came closer to Lucius so he could see the intricate working of silver and green enamel. 'It was made by a craftsman of the Decantae, to the north,' Calgacus explained. 'He lived on the shore of a long, very deep lake in that country.

He told my father that the monstrous creature he crafted here on black stone is real, and lives inside the lake. He swore he'd seen it on moonlit nights. My father laughed when he heard this, and I laughed, too, when my father told it to me. Such monsters, so we both thought, could not exist outside of legend. And so I still believe... But today, our people are faced by a monster far more deadly than this lake creature. And it comes at us like a many-headed beast, with phalanxes* of sharpened steel, and shield walls, and ballistae** that smash our defences.... To beat you, my young friend, we're going to have to learn to fight like you. I watched the three of you last night. You didn't just show skill with the sword, you showed discipline, teamwork, and between you you killed dozens of my men. That's the other reason I spared you. I want you to train my men to fight the way you do – not as individuals, but as a unit. If you'll do that for me, I'll give you lodgings in the village, and even return you your armour and weapons. What do you say?'

'Teach your men to kill Romans?' cried Quin. 'Are you mad? I would never stoop to such a betrayal.'

'But don't you realise your leaders have betrayed *you*?' Calgacus responded with equal force. 'They've brought you to a place where you don't belong. Exposed you to danger and death – for what? To win glory for themselves back in Rome.' He clasped Quin

* *phalanxes: massed formations of infantrymen.*

** *ballistae: siege catapults.*

by the shoulders. 'Join us!' he urged. 'We have justice on our side. We fight for freedom, not conquest. You're a great warrior. If you join with us, you can win *real* glory. You could become a legend!'

Quin shrugged him off. 'Never!' he hissed.

Calgacus nodded sadly, then spoke a few words to the guard standing next to Quin. The guard hauled Quin through the animal-hide curtain and out of the building.

Lucius stared after them fearfully, then spun round to face Calgacus. 'Will you kill him?' he asked.

The chieftain chuckled and shook his head. 'No, but I can make his life miserable enough. A few days of starvation rations should bring him to his senses... But what about you, young man? You seem more sensible. Will you help us?'

Lucius shook his head. 'I cannot,' he said. 'Like my brother, I am first of all a Roman. Whatever you think of us, I know we're better than that. I just wish you'd give us a chance to prove it to you.'

'I don't doubt you speak from the heart, young soldier. But your offer of citizenship – to us it sounds a lot like slavery. If you really want to help us, teach us how to fight.'

In the chieftain's grey eyes Lucius glimpsed sadness, but also an unbreakable strength of purpose, and he understood how this man could have united the tribes under his leadership. Yet, however charismatic he was, Calgacus would never be able to break Lucius's own tribal loyalty to Rome.

'No,' he said.

Calgacus looked down, disappointed.

'I'll help you,' said Isi.

Lucius turned sharply towards her, shocked.

'The quiet one speaks,' said Calgacus with a smile.

'I'll teach you all I know,' said Isi, 'if you promise to treat my brothers well.'

'That could be arranged,' said Calgacus, nodding slowly.

'No!' Lucius shouted at her. 'You can't!'

But Isi didn't even look at him.

Calgacus issued an instruction to the guards, and Lucius felt powerful hands close tightly around his arms. As he was dragged from the round house, he gave full vent to his fury: 'Traitor!' he yelled at Isi. 'I'll never speak to you again!'

CHAPTER VII

26–27 MAY

I t was approaching evening by the time Lucius emerged from the round house. Wood for a bonfire had been placed in the clearing at the centre of the village in preparation for the evening feast. Villagers ceased their gossiping when they caught sight of Lucius, but soon resumed it as he was shoved along the path and pushed back into the cage. He found Quin there, prowling around like a restless tiger. 'Where's Isi?' Quin demanded.

'She's agreed to help them,' said Lucius with a sag of his shoulders.

'What?' snarled Quin. 'I don't believe it! The traitor! The backstabber!'

Lucius sank to the floor, leaned back against the cage wall and ran his hands wearily through his hair.

'She's Egyptian, remember – not Roman. I think she feels a sort of... kinship with these people. Fellow sufferers under the Roman yoke, that sort of thing.'

'Ah, that's a load of tosh!' said Quin. 'She's Roman to her fingertips. She's lived there practically all her life. The Egyptian thing is just an act – a pose. When she actually went there and saw what a dump it was, she didn't stay long, did she? She owes everything to Rome, and this is how she pays her city back – by giving away all our secrets.' He ran to the cage wall and began pounding the basketwork wall. 'Traitor!' he cried. 'Double-crosser! Renegade!'

'Calm down,' said Lucius. 'It won't do any good.'

Quin began kicking at the sticks at the base of the cage – repeatedly kicking and kicking as a way of releasing all his frustration. Suddenly they both heard a crack. Quin looked down and saw that one of the more slender of the horizontal branches that bound the vertical stakes had partially snapped. After glancing around to check that no one from the village or the palisade was watching, he kicked at it some more. Several more blows from the tip of his sandal were enough to split the branch in two.

'Careful, Quin,' whispered Lucius, glancing anxiously towards the village where people were gathering for the feast. 'We should wait until dark – it's too risky now.'

But Quin was already on his knees, using all his strength to force two of the vertical stakes apart, trying to create enough space for them to wriggle through.

'Help me!' he gasped.

Lucius shrugged and got down into a crouch beside his brother. He leaned back, using his weight to pull one of the stakes leftwards, while Quin put all his weight into pulling the other one to the right. The ropes binding the stakes to the lateral branches began to creak. The stakes shifted, and gradually a sizeable gap was formed. Quin lay down flat on his stomach and pushed his head and arms into the gap, shoving, squirming and wriggling to get his body through.

Lucius was getting seriously worried. If a single guard were to look up at that moment, they would be caught and probably killed. And how did they hope to scale the palisade and get away? It was a crazy idea. 'Quin!' he whispered hoarsely. 'Stop! Let's not do this now. We should make a plan.'

But Quin didn't stop. Having got himself through the gap, he turned back to his brother. 'It's now or never, Lu! Are you coming?'

Lucius looked towards the village. The bonfire had been lit. The villagers had gathered there, and food was being served. They were oblivious to everything else. He scanned the palisade. To his right, he saw some guards carrying torches. A couple of them had spotted Quin and were now running towards the cage.

'It's too late!' cried Lucius. 'We've been spotted.'

Quin's jaw was set. 'Farewell then, brother!' he said, rising to his feet and racing off in the opposite direction from the pursuing guards, making for an unguarded part of the palisade.

His heart hammering in his chest, Lucius watched Quin sprint towards the high wooden wall that surrounded the settlement. 'Come on!' he murmured under his breath. 'You can do it!'

Staying low to the ground, Quin ran past outbuildings and grain stores. When he reached the palisade, he took a flying leap at the platform that ran around its inner side. The platform was close to the top of the palisade, some eight or nine feet* above the ground. Quin managed to grab on to it with his fingertips. He clung there helplessly for a few seconds, before finding the strength to swing his legs forward and clamp his thighs around one of the timber struts that supported the platform. Meanwhile, guards were closing in on the escaped prisoner, hurrying towards him along the platform in both directions, their flaming torches vivid against the purple sky.

'Quick!' Lucius urged him. 'You're nearly there!'

Quin hoisted himself up onto the platform, then bolted towards the top of the palisade. He grasped two of the sharpened stakes and launched himself upwards, trying to vault right over them. But in the middle of this acrobatic leap, he was grabbed by a guard and dragged backwards. Three more guards then piled in, and together they forced Quin down onto the platform's timber floor.

* *eight or nine (Roman) feet: 2.4–2.7 metres.*

Lucius bashed the ground in frustration. His brother had come within a whisker of escaping. Now he could only watch as Quin was escorted down a ladder and along the path to the village. Lucius was seriously worried that Baltair would now get his way and be allowed to kill Quin – after all, Calgacus could no longer argue that Quin might be useful to them.

Lucius shivered as a cold wind whipped in from the mountains. He drew his cloak tighter around his body. Footsteps approached and he looked up, hoping it was Quin. But it was only an old carpenter who'd come to fix the hole they'd made in the cage wall. As he went to work, the thickly bearded man cursed Lucius in what sounded like colourful language, but Lucius just let the meaningless noise wash over him. He laid himself down on the ground and hugged his knees. It was always cold in this wretched land. He closed his eyes and let his mind drift back to a sunny afternoon on the Esquiline Hill – Argos barking at him, begging to be taken for a walk – as if Lucius needed any persuasion! He remembered the two of them visiting the Temple of Juno Lucina* – and getting chased away by an elderly Vestal Virgin** after Argos had decided to use a 500-year-old lotus tree in the temple's sacred grove as a lavatory. Lucius smiled at the memory, and his heart ached because he missed his dog so much.

* *Juno Lucina: goddess of childbirth.*

** *Vestal Virgin: a priestess of Vesta, the goddess of the hearth. The Vestals looked after the lotus trees and hung offerings on them.*

An hour later, Quin returned. He staggered into the cage and collapsed, groaning. He was wearing only his cloak and a loincloth underneath. He carried his tunic bundled up in his arms. Lucius was overjoyed to see his brother alive, but scared to imagine what they'd done to him. The red stains he could see on the cream-coloured tunic only increased his alarm.

'Are you OK?' he asked.

Quin's breath came in shuddering gasps. 'I didn't make a sound,' he croaked. 'Not a single sound.'

Lucius approached him, frightened now. He drew back Quin's cloak.

His back was a mass of angry red welts. They must have flogged him at least thirty times.

Lucius let the cloak fall. 'There's blood on your lip, too,' he observed.

'That was my doing,' said Quin, with a red-toothed smile. 'I'd sooner chew off my own lip than give them the pleasure of hearing me scream.'

'I'm sorry,' said Lucius.

'It's OK,' grunted Quin. 'It was my choice to try and escape. And I'll do it again, soon as I get the chance. If they want to keep me here, they'll have to kill me first.'

Lucius fetched his brother a ladleful of water, which Quin gratefully drank. 'Rest now,' said Lucius, patting his shoulder. 'We'll think up a new plan in the morning.'

Lucius returned to his own side of the cage and tried to settle down to sleep. But the feast in the village was in full swing – the enormous bonfire cast a homely orange glow over the settlement – and it was especially hard to ignore the delicious food smells wafting in on the breeze, along with sounds of laughter and singing.

Eventually, he gave up trying to sleep and sat up and watched the villagers party. As he sat there, he was surprised to see the silhouette of a female figure approach along the path. As she drew closer, he saw it was Floree, bringing them some fresh water.

Upon entering the cage, she put down the bucket and scampered over to Quin, kneeling down beside his slumped figure. Lucius pretended to be asleep, watching through half-closed eyes as she pulled aside Quin's cloak. Floree gasped as she took in the wounds on his back. From within the folds of her dress, she drew out a small clay vessel – a healing ointment, Lucius guessed – and a cloth. He heard Quin groan as she began gently dabbing the wounds. Quin twisted around, and his eyes widened when he saw who it was. Floree put a finger to her lips and turned his head back to the ground so she could concentrate on treating him.

Eventually, Lucius nodded off. At some point during the night, he may have woken up and seen Floree and Quin kissing. Then again, it may have been a dream – he couldn't be sure.

She certainly wasn't there when morning finally arrived. Lucius yawned and stretched, trying to get some feeling back into his stiff limbs. For an angry moment he thought of Isi, waking up in a comfy bed in one of those snug little round houses. He hoped she spared a guilty thought for him and Quin.

He had a drink of water, swilling it around his mouth and spitting it out. Then he helped himself to a chunk of yesterday's bread. Quin, he noticed, was awake, rubbing his eyes and grimacing with discomfort.

'So how was *your* night?' Lucius asked innocently – he decided not to mention what he'd witnessed.

'It was all right,' yawned Quin, not quite meeting his eyes. 'Here, pass the rest of that bread, will you?'

As Quin munched on the bread, a shadow fell across him – a very large shadow. He and Lucius looked up to see Baltair standing outside the cage, flanked by a couple of henchmen – big fellows in their own right, but dwarfed by their boss. Baltair was staring at Quin, looking angrier than Lucius had ever seen him. In fact, the way his face was twitching and his fingers were flexing, he looked as if he was about to rip apart the cage wall, before ripping apart Quin. A low growling filled the air, and Lucius looked around for dogs – until he realised that the sound was actually coming from Baltair's throat. The growl eventually turned into words...

'You sleep with my daughter,' said Baltair

menacingly. 'Her little brother see you two last night. He tell me this morning he see you with Floree.'

So Floree was Baltair's daughter! Lucius almost groaned aloud when he heard this. Of all the women Quin could have chosen for a girlfriend...

Quin climbed painfully to his feet and faced Baltair. 'I didn't know she was your daughter,' he said. 'But yes, it's true, she was here last night.'

'You bring shame and dishonour to my family,' said Baltair, his hands squeezing down on the bars of the cage. 'Now I must kill you. Calgacus will not stand in my way. Then, when I have killed you, I will kill Floree.'

Lucius saw the shock and distress on Quin's face as he heard these last words. 'Kill me if you wish,' he cried. 'But don't hurt Floree. She is completely innocent.'

'You not tell me what I must do with my daughter!' snarled Baltair, bashing the cage wall with his fists. 'She must die. It is the only way to restore honour. But first, I kill you.'

With that, he marched to the cage door, unbolted it and flung it open. Quin backed off as the giant drew his huge iron sword and swung it in a wide circle above his head. 'Prepare to die, Roman!' he thundered.

'Not so fast, Baltair!'

Everyone turned to see Calgacus standing outside the cage looking in.

Baltair turned on his leader and bellowed his

fury at him in words Lucius was grateful he couldn't understand.

Calgacus's expression didn't change during the tirade. When it was over, he turned to Quin. 'Baltair claims that this dispute between the two of you concerns his family's personal honour. It has nothing to do with the tribe, so I, as tribal chief, cannot stand in his way.' He then returned his attention to the giant. 'That may be true, Baltair,' he said, 'but as leader of this village, I certainly do have a say on how blood is to be shed on its soil.' He allowed himself a modest smile as an idea appeared to occur to him. 'I propose a fight to the death,' said Calgacus. 'We can hold it this very evening. Single combat, with weapons of your own choosing. If Baltair wins, he gets back his honour. If the Roman wins, well…'

'The Roman won't win,' spat Baltair.

'No,' chuckled Calgacus, 'I don't suppose he will. Remind me how many single combats you've fought, Baltair?'

'Twenty-five,' growled the giant, his red-rimmed eyes remaining fastened on Quin.

'And how many of those have you won?'

'Twenty-five.'

Calgacus laughed as he sauntered back to the village. 'Good luck, Roman!' he called over his shoulder. 'I think you may need it.'

'Quin, what have you done?' Lucius asked despairingly, when they were alone again.

'How was I to know she was his daughter?' replied Quin, looking at his feet.

'He *will* kill you, you know.'

'I've been in worse fixes than this and survived,' said Quin grimly.

'Such as?'

'Remember the Mesopotamian Lion?'

Lucius recalled Quin's famous slaying of the lion at the Flavian Amphitheatre two years earlier. It was his speed and agility that had won him victory that day, but he didn't exactly look fast or agile now – not with the injuries to his back.

Quin may have seen the doubt in Lucius's face as he sought to give further reassurance to him – or perhaps to himself. 'I was thinking only of my own survival that day,' he said. 'This time, I have a much greater motivation – I'm doing this to save Floree.'

'I thought you were joking when you said you were in love with her,' said Lucius. 'Do you really care that much for the girl?'

Colour came into Quin's cheeks. 'I don't know…' he said. 'I felt something when I first set eyes on her, and I think she did, too.' He turned away. 'I realise we're worlds apart' he said. 'We can hardly even understand each other. But if I can save her life, that would be something…'

'You mean by killing her father,' said Lucius.

Quin bit his bloodstained lip. 'I can't imagine she has much love for a man who's prepared to kill her over this.'

Lucius observed the certainty in his brother's face, and was troubled by it. Quin seemed completely convinced that he was doing the right thing for Floree – that he was the gallant hero coming to her rescue – but he knew nothing about these people or their ways.

'You say you want to win this fight to save her life,' said Lucius, 'but you have no idea what kind of life you'd be consigning her to. She's already disgraced in their eyes. If you kill Baltair, she'll be fatherless, and most probably cast out by her tribe.'

Quin absorbed this with a thoughtful nod. 'I can't risk that,' he said finally. 'If I win this fight, I'll just have to take her away with me.'

CHAPTER VIII

27 MAY

Calgacus's chief guard offered Quin one of his tribe's long, heavy iron swords to do battle with. This would put Quin on slightly more equal terms with Baltair in terms of reach and power of strike (although the giant's longer arms and bigger muscles would ensure his overall superiority in these areas). After giving it some thought, Quin decided to opt instead for his trusty gladius. He knew he would struggle to handle the bigger weapon, and it would reduce the one possible advantage he might have against the bigger man – speed. The gladius, on the other hand, had become almost like a part of his body over the past week of intensive training – a sharp, quick and deadly extension to his right arm.

The sky turned grey during the morning, sending down a cold misty drizzle that shrouded the settlement like an evil wet cloak. Quin was given leave to practise with his sword in the hours leading up to the fight, which was scheduled for the late afternoon. Wearing nothing but his loincloth and a pair of borrowed Caledonian leggings, Quin diligently went through his manoeuvres in the cage, cutting and thrusting at an imaginary palus* until his back became too painful to continue. When that happened, he would lie on his stomach while Lucius treated his wounds with some of the healing ointment left behind by Floree. The only break in this routine was lunch – rain-sodden bread and a few scraps of wild boar – which the brothers ate seated opposite each other, cross-legged, as the drizzle turned the earth around them into soft, sticky mud.

The rain finally ceased in the latter part of the day and a low sun broke through the cloud cover in the western sky. A sense of dread settled over Lucius's heart as he watched the villagers gather once again in the central space that functioned as a forum for their little community. This time they were coming to witness what they all saw as Baltair's justified quest to restore honour to his family name, and the confident smiles on their ruddy faces showed exactly how they expected the afternoon's events to unfold.

Once everyone had taken their places, the guards finally came for Lucius and Quin. Following his

---

* palus: a wooden post used as a target for sword practice.

brother along the path into the village, Lucius noticed that Quin walked with the same confident swagger he displayed every time he entered a gladiatorial arena. It was a confidence based on nothing that Lucius could put his finger on, except perhaps a belief in his own extraordinary destiny.

As Quin entered the roped-off space set aside for the fight, Lucius was forcibly held back by two of the guards. They held him firmly by the wrists and forced him to kneel by the edge of the little arena, no doubt concerned that he might try and take advantage of the distraction caused by the fight to attempt an escape. Looking around him, he saw that the entire village had turned out to witness the fight, from mothers with babes in their arms to elderly folk with bent bodies supported by gnarled sticks. This was, he imagined, a rare chance for this cowed and demoralised people to enjoy the sight of a Roman being brought down by one of their own native fighters.

Baltair was already waiting there in the ring, looking impatient for the fight to commence. If anything, he seemed even bigger than before. The muscles in his bare torso bulged, rippled and coiled like angry sea serpents. His shoulders and arms resembled the quivering limbs of an ancient oak tree in a high wind as he swished and twirled his huge sword above his head.

Quin allowed his cloak to fall from his shoulders, revealing his own impressive upper body. Yet to everyone present it was immediately obvious how mismatched the two were, at least in size. Baltair stood more than a head taller and had a body and limbs easily twice the diameter of his opponent's. The crowd reacted with merciless cheers and laughter to the sight of the wounds on Quin's back.

On the far side of the arena was Calgacus, seated on a wooden throne set upon an elevated platform, with his retinue of guards standing behind him. He shared the platform with the four other visiting tribal leaders Lucius had seen the day before, two on either side of him. With a shudder of angry disappointment, Lucius spotted Isi to the right of the platform. The low sun shone on her face, marking her out from the rest of the crowd, as if she weren't distinctive enough already with her olive-brown skin and jet-black hair. Her face was impassive, like the mask of one of the ancient embalmed kings of her homeland. She looked neither at Lucius nor at Quin, but straight ahead. Did she feel any guilt at all? He wondered what was going on behind those enigmatic brown eyes. Next to her stood Juvenius – two traitors to Rome. What a fine pair they made! At least Juvenius had the decency to keep his eyes lowered in shame.

There was a movement to Lucius's left and another prisoner was brought to the ringside. It was Floree. She was in the clutches of a pair of guards, who forced her to her knees beside Lucius. Her cheeks were blotchy from crying, yet she held her head proud and erect. Like Quin displaying his wounds for all to see, she seemed unashamed of herself or her actions. Lucius was impressed by her bravery – perhaps she and Quin did belong together after all. But the chorus of jeers that her appearance provoked suggested that the crowd didn't share Lucius's high opinion of her – they probably interpreted her proud look as evidence of her shameless and immoral character.

Baltair, who had been twirling and swashing his sword as if it were made of something far lighter than iron, stopped when he caught sight of his daughter. His face immediately contorted into a look of hatred and he began spewing what sounded like foul curses in her direction. Floree flinched, almost as if she were being struck in the face, but refused to look down.

Then it was Quin's turn to bear the brunt of Baltair's tongue. 'You, Roman,' he snarled in his rudimentary Latin, lowering his sword until it was pointing at Quin's throat. 'You dishonour me and my kin. Now I make you pay! I will kill you like I have killed every man who disrespects me. I will slaughter you like a pig. And when you are dead I will cut off your head and all of your limbs and deliver them to your General Agricola so he will know what happens to a Roman who dares to dishonour Baltair!'

Calgacus spoke a few words in the native tongue, then signalled for the fight to begin. Quin raised his sword so that it was level with Baltair's much longer one, and the two began to circle. Above them the clouds hung dark and menacing, and the low sun shone out of the west, its silver light glinting cruelly off the razor edge of Baltair's blade. Quin was semi-crouched with head tilted upwards, unblinking eyes fixed on his opponent as he edged around the circumference of an imaginary circle, just out of range of the giant's blade. Baltair suddenly stepped forward and swung, his blade whistling through the air towards Quin's left flank. A swift shuffle of the feet and a twist of the body, and Quin met the incoming attack with a block. The clash of iron on steel rang sharply through the air, drawing gasps. Baltair attacked again, this time from the right. Again, Quin was ready with a block – and a second later he had to raise his sword to deflect an even more powerful chop from above. Despite his size and the weight of his sword, Baltair was quick, with each successive blow coming too fast for Quin to even consider a counterstrike.

Lucius was close enough to the action to see the beads of sweat flying off his brother's face, and the ripples that ran through his body as it absorbed the shock of each successive hammer-blow. He could see how vulnerable Quin's flesh was, unprotected by manica, greave* or shield, and how death or dismemberment seemed to come closer with every incoming sweep of that giant blade.

And the blows didn't stop coming. Lucius quickly saw that Baltair was the type of fighter who disdained

* *manica: shoulder guard; greave: leg guard.*

tactics or subtlety – he liked to bludgeon his opponents into submission, attacking and attacking and attacking until, through sheer dizziness or exhaustion, their defences opened up and he could execute the killing blow. The blows continued to rain down on Quin from all sides – from left and right, above and below. Sometimes Baltair would vary it, attacking twice or even three times from the same direction to try and catch Quin out. And the blows came so fast, it was impossible for Quin to do anything except react. The former gladiator had to move quicker than he ever had before, dancing back and forth, side to side, swinging his sword one way, then the other, blocking, parrying and deflecting – under such an onslaught, his sword had become nothing more than a very narrow shield.

As the fight wore on, Quin's turns and blocks became ever more desperate, and the edge of Baltair's sword penetrated closer and closer to its vulnerable target. Quin's gasps were audible as he whirled around to block an attack to his rear, then arched upwards to defend himself from an assault on his head. The guttural cries and roars of the crowd increased in volume as they sensed Baltair closing in on his opponent's flesh. Lucius watched it all, mouth open, ears ringing with each metallic clang. All thought disappeared from his mind – he almost forgot to breathe as he became fixated on the lethal motions of Baltair's sword.

Glancing momentarily to his left, Lucius noticed that Floree had her hands clasped over her mouth. Her cheeks were ghostly pale as her staring, tear-filled eyes followed the progress of the two figures in the arena. Lucius couldn't even guess at the emotions washing through her at that moment. If she loved Quin, and her own life, then she must be desperately scared that she was about to lose both. On the other hand, could she really wish for a reversal of the situation, with her own father facing death, however cruel he was?

The sound of a skid and a stumble jerked Lucius's attention back to the arena. Quin had fallen. He was on his back. Baltair was towering over him, his blade plummeting down. Quin rolled at the last minute, and Baltair's sword bit soft earth. By the time he had pulled it free, Quin was back on his feet and had managed to duck in close enough to take a swing of his own. A line of crimson appeared across Baltair's thigh. The crowd lurched with surprise, emitting a grunt as if they'd been punched collectively in the stomach. There were shouts of anger. They'd been preparing to cheer victory – how dare the Roman spoil things with this cowardly counterstrike? But the villagers quickly recovered their spirits as they saw the thick smile spreading across Baltair's lips. The wound was light – it was nothing. Everything was still fine…

Nevertheless, a thin shaft of hope had broken through the blanket of dread that had enveloped Lucius – Quin had inflicted first blood, however minor the wound was, and that might just introduce a worm of uncertainty into Baltair's mind. But if Baltair felt any such doubts, he hid them very well as he recommenced his pummelling attack. Several times he forced Quin to retreat to the very edge of the roped-off area and almost into the crowd, as he battered him with repeated sword blows. But each time Quin ran out of space and looked about to be skewered, he somehow managed to wriggle his way clear, forcing Baltair to turn round and start advancing on him once again. Baltair smiled his way through each of these little setbacks, but the crowd began to notice that the big man's breathing was getting heavier and rivulets of sweat were pouring off his large head like mountain streams. Even the great pounding strikes from his sword seemed to be dropping off in power and frequency. Could Baltair be getting tired? Had Quin weathered the storm?

Serious alarm broke out in the crowd as Quin found a way through Baltair's defences a second time, slicing a bloody gash just above his adversary's hip. There was no smile from Baltair this time. Instead, his face creased in pain and frustration, his eyes darkened, and he roared like a bear. He charged at Quin, sword twirling. Quin sidestepped and brought the flat of his gladius down hard against Baltair's lower leg. Baltair fell forwards into the crowd, very nearly crushing some young boys, who only just managed to get out of the way in time.

The crowd emitted a sickly groan. They had never seen their champion humbled like this. There were a few seconds, as Baltair struggled clumsily to his feet, when Quin had the opportunity for a killing strike to his back, but Quin refused to take advantage. Instead, he retreated to the centre of the arena until his opponent was ready to resume. Floree's hands had dropped back to her lap. Her lips were parted, and fresh blooms of colour had appeared on her cheeks. Quin's sportsmanship provoked one or two murmurs of surprise. The majority, however, were perturbed, unsettled, and verging on hysteria. Lucius sensed danger, but more from the villagers than from Baltair, who seemed a shrunken, more uncertain figure as he resumed the fight against Quin. The people of the village were angry. They were yelling at Baltair, and it wasn't clear to Lucius whether they were trying to encourage him or blaming him for his failure.

An elderly man suddenly hobbled into the ring and whacked Quin hard over the head with his walking stick, sending him crashing to the ground. The crowd laughed and stamped their feet. Baltair joined in the laughter. With a resurgence of his old energy he raised his sword, arching his body to deliver a sweeping cut that would take Quin's head clean off. Lucius screamed at his brother to move, but Quin, dazed by the blow, remained on all fours beneath Baltair's sword, head flopped forward. Lucius could hear Floree's sobs. He screamed again, and as he did so something extremely bright flashed in his eyes, momentarily blinding him. Whatever it was must have blinded Baltair, too, because the giant was standing just a few paces in front of

Lucius, facing the same way. Baltair took a backward step, and moved his forearm across his eyes to block out the glare. When he brought his sword down a few seconds later, Quin was no longer there. Quin had staggered to his feet, and before Baltair could raise his sword again, he thrust his gladius deep into the giant's side. The great warrior groaned. He opened his mouth in surprise and blood trickled down his lower lip. The crowd was silenced and their laughing faces changed to looks of horror. Baltair's sword fell from his fingers. His eyes clouded and he sank slowly to his knees as blood poured freely from his side, staining his leggings. For a long time he remained in a kneeling position, looking strangely peaceful, like someone at prayer. Then he fell forward, and his face hit the earth.

In the confused seconds that followed, Lucius – and probably most other people – were too busy trying to work out what had just happened to react. What *had* just happened? What was that blinding light that had distracted Baltair just as he was about to behead Quin? Whatever it was, it had changed everything, because Baltair was now dead, and Quin was standing over his body, looking as confused as everyone else. It couldn't have been the sun because the sun was behind Lucius's head, and this light had come from the opposite direction…

And that was when Lucius remembered a story his father had once told him about the famous Greek scientist Archimedes, who had made a 'burning glass'.

When this glass faced the sun, the sun's power was so magnified that it destroyed a Roman fleet. The burning glass had been a mirror. Lucius scrutinised the area where he thought the light had come from. Isi was standing there, bathed in sunlight, her face still as impassive as a pharaoh's mask. Had *she* been responsible? Then he saw something in her hand – most of it was hidden beneath her cloak, but he saw enough to recognise it as the handle of the bronze mirror belonging to her mother... *Of course!* Held at the right angle, that highly polished surface would have produced a reflection almost as bright as the sun itself. He wanted to run over and give her a hug, apologise for thinking badly of her, and thank her for her quick thinking. Her mirror hadn't destroyed a fleet, but it had helped destroy Baltair, and in Lucius's opinion that gave it legendary status.

Floree was the first among her fellow villagers to move. She ran to Baltair's lifeless body and embraced it, her shoulders heaving with sobs, her auburn hair forming a curtain across his great shoulders. This caused a stir in the crowd, and Lucius thought he detected a few expressions of sympathy. Certainly, no one could have expected such a show of filial grief from the disgraced girl, considering how her father had wanted her dead. But the majority remained angry and bitter at the defeat and death of their hero. Many shouted their fury at Quin. A group of boys even began pelting him with rotten vegetables. Quin backed out of range of this artillery fire, only to find himself getting attacked from behind by a pack of aggressive middle-aged women. They punched and kicked him with surprising violence, and their assault was only brought to an end by a shouted command from Calgacus.

The chieftain strode into the ring, and the women and boys immediately backed off. Calgacus walked up to Quin, grasped the wrist of his sword hand and raised it aloft. Shocked and angry murmurs rippled through the crowd at this surprising acknowledgement of the Roman's victory. Calgacus frowned at these subversive mutterings. He released Quin's arm, and approached the angriest section of the crowd. He spoke to them slowly and calmly, and the murmuring and grumbling gradually diminished – though Lucius could see that many remained unhappy.

When Calgacus had finished speaking to them, he turned back to Quin. 'You fought bravely and well,' he said. 'Baltair was not the noblest of men, but he was our most formidable fighter, and you defeated him. You have refused to be our teacher, Roman, but in your own way you taught us some invaluable lessons today. You taught us that good defensive fighting can withstand the most ferocious assault, and that swiftness in the strike can overcome a much larger foe. I should remember that next time I face the might of your legions. When our young men have got over their disappointment, I'm convinced they will re-stage your extraordinary performance many times over with their wooden swords, and your lessons will be absorbed by the next generation… You have earned your freedom today, Roman. Of course, I would be delighted if you would stay with us and teach us more of your skills. I know you've formed an attachment to Baltair's daughter. If I cannot induce you to stay, then perhaps she can… But, if you and your brother insist upon leaving, I will not stand in your way.'

Lucius nearly laughed with delight at these words. *They were free!*… Yet there was something that nagged at him in Calgacus's words: he'd said 'brother', when surely he'd meant 'brothers'.

'Thank you,' said Quin. 'Your offer is tempting, but I still wish to return to my people.' He paused, before adding: 'Though you seem to have forgotten that I have two brothers.'

As he said this, Isi stepped into the ring and approached Quin. 'I'm not going with you,' she said softly.

Lucius started towards her. 'Isi!' he cried. 'What are you saying?'

'I think this is where I belong, Lucius,' she said, and he saw that her eyes were damp and red from crying. 'I feel a fellowship with these people. I understand their struggle. I'm sorry. I just wish you could see the world as I do.'

'No, Isi!'

She hugged him tight. 'My dearest wish', she said,

'would be for you to stay here with me.'

For a brief, mad moment, Lucius imagined himself living in this hilltop village, taking up a trade, living next door to Isi, growing old among these people. Quin would be there, too, married to Floree. There was something quite comforting about the vision...

Then he returned to his senses. He was a Roman. He was here in Caledonia on a mission to destroy his enemy and restore his family's name. If he was to grow old anywhere it would be on the Esquiline Hill in Rome, living in the house of his ancestors.

His voice sank to a whisper. 'You have to come with us, Isi. This isn't why we came here. You were going to help us find Parmenion, remember?'

She shook her head, eyes shining with tears but also with the light of certainty. 'I was awake all last night thinking about it,' she said, 'and I've realised that it must have been destiny that brought me here, not Parmenion. I wish you luck with your quest. I know you'll succeed and that one day you'll be reunited with your mother and sister in your lovely house.'

'I wanted you to be there, too,' he groaned, almost to himself. Then he pulled himself together. 'I'll miss you,' he said.

'I'll miss you, too,' she replied. He felt eyes upon him, and turned to see Calgacus looking at them with a puzzled expression. He supposed they didn't look much like brothers at that moment. Reluctantly, he and Isi parted from each other.

Meanwhile, Quin was embracing Floree, trying to give her comfort, though he had no words she would understand. He asked Calgacus: 'What will happen to Floree now?'

'I will adopt her as my daughter,' the chief said. 'There are a few die-hard traditionalists in the village who, like her late father, will want to see her killed for sleeping with a Roman. Of course I disagree with this view, and as long as I remain alive, I will keep her safe.'

Quin had no choice but to accept this guarantee from Calgacus. Lucius sensed that his brother was tempted to carry Floree away with him – impulsive, romantic soul that he was – but even Quin had to accept that a legionary camp was no place for a Caledonian woman. He would have to content himself with the knowledge that he'd saved her life.

Lucius and Quin departed the village the following morning. Isi, Calgacus and Floree were there to see them off. Calgacus pointed to a river that wound its way along the valley beneath. He told the brothers to follow the course of the river downstream, and they would arrive at Pinnata by evening. He urged them to refrain from telling their Roman masters the location of the village. Quin and Lucius promised that it would remain their secret. With Isi and Floree living there, they had every reason to keep that promise.

'I don't suppose I can persuade you to change your mind,' Lucius said to Isi.

'Go!' she commanded, 'before I start crying again.'

Lucius and Quin began making their way down the narrow track. When they reached the valley floor, Lucius turned and looked back towards the hilltop palisade. Calgacus had gone back inside the village, but the two women were still there by the gate, watching them go.

CHAPTER IX

28 MAY

s Calgacus had predicted, they made it back to Pinnata Castra just as the light began to fade from the sky. For several miles before that, they had seen columns of smoke rising through the trees on the horizon – which they had assumed to be the remains of the fires lit by the Caledonian attackers three nights earlier – and they feared what they would find when they arrived.

But Pinnata Castra turned out not to be an abandoned, smoke-blackened ruin – far from it: the place was a hive of activity, a veritable construction site filled with teams of stonemasons, carpenters, brickmakers, blacksmiths and engineers. The fort was being rebuilt even stronger than before, with stouter defences and with stone and brick replacing timber as the main construction materials. The smoke plumes they'd seen on the horizon had come from mobile kilns where bricks were being fired for the new walls.

After identifying themselves to the sentries at the gate, Lucius and Quin had a wash in the bathhouse, then made their way to the crowded mess hall where hundreds of soldiers were sitting down for their evening meal. The vast majority of the faces looked unfamiliar to them. From some legionaries sitting nearby, they learned that General Agricola was now back in residence, having returned hotfoot from the northeast as soon as he'd heard about the attack. He had arrived at the head of almost three thousand men, bringing the camp back up to full strength. Lucius prayed that Parmenion was among the newly arrived force.

When they had finished their meal, he and Quin made their way to Gallicus's quarters in the principia, planning to report their arrival to the training instructor. He wasn't there, however, and neither was there any sign of their fellow munifices. So they went to Verres's office in the same building to report to him instead.

Verres was in the middle of dictating something to a scribe when they came in. He looked up vaguely, then did a double-take when he saw who it was. 'Well, if it isn't the Galerii boys... minus one. And there was I thinking you were dead. What happened?'

'We were captured...' began Quin.

'But we escaped before they could take us wherever they were taking us,' added Lucius.

They had rehearsed their story on the journey.

'It took us a couple of days to find our way back here,' finished Quin.

Verres didn't appear very interested in their adventure.

'Excellent,' he said. 'I'm glad you're all right. Now if you'll excuse me I really must get on. The administrative task of catering for a sudden influx of three thousand men is quite a challenge, as I'm sure you can imagine.'

'We didn't plan on disturbing you,' said Quin. 'We were just wondering where Centurion Gallicus was, and the rest of our contubernium.'*

'All dead, I'm afraid,' sighed Verres. 'Either axed or burned to death in the attack on the barrack blocks – as I assumed you were, too.'

'You didn't try to identify the bodies, then?' asked Lucius, a bit dismayed by Verres's offhand attitude.

'There was little chance of identifying anyone among the piles of charred bones we found the next morning,' said Verres. 'If you'd like to bid farewell to your former chums, they're currently dumping them by the sackload in the river. What happened to your brother, by the way? The quiet one.'

'He's probably in one of the sacks they're dumping in the river,' said Quin.

* contubernium: a squad of eight men.

'I see,' said Verres. 'Well, I'm sorry for your loss. Now, if there's nothing else…' He turned back to the scribe.

'Do you know if Parmenion was among those who came back with General Agricola?' asked Lucius.

Verres frowned. 'I'm not sure,' he said. 'I've yet to receive the records of all the new arrivals. Perhaps if you call back tomorrow morning…'

The door suddenly swung open and a senior officer swept into the room. Lucius recognised him as the camp's military tribune, Appius Mallius Lurco. He looked immaculate in his gleaming bronze breastplate moulded to show chest and stomach muscles, and his scarlet cloak pinned to his right shoulder by a fancy jewelled clasp. Even in this flashy attire, the man was not exactly an imposing individual, being short, with weak limbs, a pale 'indoor' complexion and a balding head. Yet there was something rather haughty about the disdainful curl of his mouth and the way he looked down his nose at Lucius and Quin. He seemed to Lucius exactly like one of those types who had gained his rank through luck of birth rather than prowess on the battlefield – for such men of noble family, the role of military tribune was a mere stepping stone in their climb up the political ladder. From the look of Lurco's smooth, unblemished complexion and perfectly clean armour, Lucius guessed he hadn't played a major role in the defence of the fort three nights ago.

Lurco soon switched his attention to Verres. 'Have

you done that inventory report for me yet, Optio Verres?' he asked in a voice that sounded like honey mixed with steel.

'Not yet, sir,' said Verres, looking more ruffled than Lucius had ever seen him. 'I've been somewhat distracted today, what with one thing and a—'

'Well, see it's on my desk by the end of the day, will you? There's a good chap.' Lurco paused on the point of exiting, looking once more at Lucius and Quin. 'Who are these two?' he asked Verres.

'Lucius and Quintus Galerius,' Verres responded. 'They were captured by the barbarians on the night of the attack, but they escaped.'

'If they've been in close quarters with the enemy then they'll need debriefing. The general will want to speak to them personally. But I'm sure you were about to see to that, weren't you, Verres?'

'I was just on the point of sending them over to you, sir,' lied Verres.

'Good,' said Lurco. 'In that case, I'll take them to the general now.'

Lucius and Quin swapped surprised glances as they followed the tribune out of Verres's office. *So they were going to meet General Agricola himself!*

For a small man, Lurco set a brisk pace, and they had to jog slightly to keep up with him as he glided down the corridor and out onto the Via Principalis. Darkness had fallen outside, yet the hammering, firing, mixing and sawing of construction did not cease.

A new shift of workmen had taken over, and would continue the work of their colleagues by torchlight through the night.

As they walked towards the praetorium, the tribune suddenly lurched to a halt and spun round. Lucius had to pull up sharp to avoid an embarrassing head-on collision.

'Galerius!' he barked. 'Now I remember... You were the fellows who were asking about Parmenion.'

'That's right, sir,' said Lucius. 'We're old friends of his. Do you happen to know if he's here at Pinnata?'

'Old friends, are you?' said Lurco, ignoring the question. 'What sort of old friends? How do you know him?' There was something very menacing and suspicious in his tone that made Lucius want to tread carefully. His mouth opened, but he felt paralysed. He hadn't planned on being asked such a question.

Then Quin jumped in with his own improvised answer: 'Before he joined up, Parmenion used to work at the Ludus Romanus where we were gladiators. He was a clerk there. That's how we got to know him.'

'I know nothing about him working at a gladiator school,' said Lurco. 'He was a scribe for the physician Diomedes before he came here.'

Lucius was astonished that the military tribune of a camp containing over five thousand men could know the personal history of one of them in such detail – unless he had a reason for taking a close interest in this particular individual.

'I mean before that, sir,' blustered Quin.

Lurco pursed his lips and nodded, but the suspicion didn't leave his eyes. 'Follow me,' he said curtly, and he turned and led them up some steps into the praetorium.

The building was among the least damaged in the camp, a few scorch marks on its stonework being the only evidence of the Caledonian attack. It was a squat, rather ugly structure with thick walls, functional columns and none of the ornamentation found in the architecture of the empire's more settled provinces. The interior was laid out around two open courts, much like the atrium and peristyle of a typical Roman house.

Lurco led them into a large room between the two courts – the equivalent of the tablinum. 'The general is currently visiting the injured in the camp hospital,' said the tribune. 'He will be back shortly. Wait here.'

Lurco departed, leaving the two of them alone in the chamber, apart from a guard who waited by the entrance. In the flickering light of the wall torches, they saw that the room was starkly furnished with a plain oak table surrounded by folding hemp-cloth chairs. The back of the room was dominated by a gigantic map covering almost the entire wall. The map showed a landmass with a ragged coastline full of inlets, bordered to the south, east and west by blue sea – the Roman province of Britannia, Lucius presumed, as accurately as Rome's geographers could depict it. The landmass was dominated by mountains in the far north, cut through by lakes and rivers. To the south of these mountains had been added a line of red dots, which Lucius took to represent the forts that Agricola was building. Among these he spotted one labelled Castra Pinnata. Arrows had been drawn to the south of the forts, presumably showing the campaigns that had won Agricola control of the lower parts of Caledonia. Here and there were scrawled the names of tribes associated with the different regions, proving that Agricola's understanding of the Caledonians was not quite so limited as Calgacus had imagined – the general knew the difference, for example, between the Damnonii and the Taexali.

At length they heard the brisk clatter of approaching soldiers, and General Gnaeus Julius Agricola, Commander of the Twentieth Legion and Proconsul* of the province of Britannia, entered the room, along with his retinue of guards.

The general was a tall man with cool, wide-spaced eyes, a prominent nose and a downturned mouth. Something about the set of his mouth and lower jaw made him appear tough, stubborn and immensely serious, and Lucius couldn't imagine the man ever relaxing or cracking a joke. In contrast with Lurco's immaculate uniform, Agricola's cloak and breastplate were dull and stained with dirt and blood. He looked as though he had just stepped off a battlefield. The general squinted frowningly at Lucius and Quin.

* *Proconsul: governor of a province of the Roman empire.*

Then Lurco emerged out of the gloom behind him, appearing as if by magic by his side.

'Sir,' he said to Agricola, 'These two young soldiers are brothers – Lucius and Quintus Galerius – and they claim to have been captured by the enemy on the night of the attack, before making their escape. They arrived back here this evening. I thought you might wish to question them.'

Agricola nodded slowly. 'What can you tell us about your captors?' he asked in a low, gravelly voice.

'Very little,' answered Lucius. 'It was dark. We travelled all through the night. Then, while they were resting their horses by a river, we managed to get away.'

'Why did they capture you, do you suppose,' probed the general, 'when, so far as I can tell, their sole aim was to inflict as much death and destruction as possible?'

'I don't know, sir,' said Lucius.

'Which direction did they take you?'

'Into the mountains northeast of here, and then into the valley beyond,' lied Quin. In fact, they had been taken along the valley that lay to the northwest.

Agricola walked past the two boys to the map that filled the rear wall. He drew his sword and traced a line with its tip heading northeast of Pinnata until he came to a river. 'Is this where you stopped?' he asked.

Quin turned to look. 'It may well have been, sir,' he said.

But Agricola's attention was no longer on the map. He was now staring hard at Quin. 'Turn around again, soldier,' he said.

Quin obeyed, turning his back to the general.

Lucius watched in horror as Agricola took three quick paces towards Quin, raised his sword and slashed at his back.

The strike was well judged, however, and didn't even graze Quin's skin. Instead, his ripped tunic fell to the floor, leaving him naked but for his loincloth. The vista of cuts, welts and bruises that marked his back was just as dense with detail as the map on the wall.

Agricola studied its mountains and valleys. 'These are recent wounds,' he observed, before turning to Lurco. 'Has this man been flogged since he's been back?'

'I'll have to check, sir...'

'I haven't,' admitted Quin.

'So your captors did this to you?' mused Agricola. 'They just stopped in the middle of their journey, did they, and decided to go to town on you with a weighted whip?'

Quin paused. 'Yes,' he said.

Agricola went very close to him. 'Don't lie to me, soldier,' he rasped, and Lucius could see flecks of his spit striking Quin's ear. 'You were taken to their encampment, weren't you? You spent time there. How else can you account for the three days it took you to travel ten miles* from that river back to here?'

Lucius could see Quin trying desperately not to crumble under the general's withering stare.

Next, Agricola turned to Lucius. 'Perhaps you'll tell me the truth, Lucius Galerius. Where were you taken? And why did you feel the need to lie to me just now?'

Lucius clenched his fist and bit down on his tongue. He felt the intensity of the general's desire for the truth – his desperation for intelligence about this mysterious enemy he was trying and failing to conquer. It was on his lips to tell Agricola everything – but then an image came to him of Isi being killed in a Roman attack on the village, and it dammed up his throat. He cursed her for putting him in this position.

'I'm sorry, sir,' he eventually spluttered, 'but it's true: my brother was beaten during the journey… that was after he tried the first time to escape. And then when we did escape, we got lost in the mountains…'

The general turned contemptuously from them both. 'Confine them to barracks,' he ordered, 'dock their pay and put them on barley rations until they're prepared to tell me what really happened.'

'Torture might prove a more expedient method of getting at the truth,' suggested Lurco.

'Just do as I say,' said Agricola, without turning round.

Lucius and Quin were escorted to one of several large dormitory tents near the perimeter wall that were

* *ten (Roman) miles: 14.8 kilometres.*

serving as temporary legionary accommodation until the new barrack blocks were built. The dormitory was filled with long rows of camp-beds containing soldiers trying to sleep against the noise of construction work outside. The boys were taken to a separate screened-off corner of the tent with a guard posted at the entrance. Lucius flung himself down on his bed, feeling the frustration of conflicting loyalties.

'I can't believe we've got ourselves into this mess,' sighed Quin, as he threw on a spare tunic and sat down on his own bed.

Lucius eyed the guard who had been assigned to them. He was half turned away from them and his attention appeared to be focused on picking pieces of greenish-yellow slime from his nose. Lucius sneaked closer to Quin's bed and seated himself on the floor near him, so they could whisper to each other.

'We have to tell Agricola something,' he said in a low voice.

'Like what?' asked Quin. 'If we point to some random spot on that map, he'll have no reason to believe us.'

'We gave Calgacus our word that we wouldn't tell anyone the location of the village, right?' murmured Lucius.

'Right,' said Quin.

'But that doesn't mean we can't report on everything else we learned while we were there – like Calgacus's uniting of the tribes, and the man's reasonable character, and how he may be open to some sort of negotiated peace. The general would be interested to hear about all that, wouldn't he?'

Quin thought about this for a moment. 'He'll still want to know where the village is,' he said.

Lucius frowned. 'What if we come clean?' he suggested. 'Tell him our brother's there and we're scared he'll be killed if the settlement's attacked. We could offer instead to go back there alone with a message from Agricola, maybe suggesting a meeting place where the two leaders could parley. You never know, the general might like that idea.'

'I suppose it's worth a try,' said Quin. He whistled at the guard to catch his attention. 'Hey! We've decided to tell all,' he said. 'Take us back to the general.'

CHAPTER X

Back in the praetorium, they were handed over to another guard, who instructed them to wait in the corridor outside the tablinum until the general had finished his meeting. The guard then went off to fetch Tribune Lurco. Quin sat down in one of the chairs provided, but Lucius sidled closer to the curtained entrance, curious to listen in to the murmured voices coming from within.

He could hear Agricola's voice, and it sounded angry. 'I received yet another letter from the emperor today,' the general fumed. 'That's the third one this month!'

'What does our Lord and God want this time?' came another voice, which Lucius recognised as belonging to the camp prefect, Decius Castus.

'Oh, the usual assurances that progress is being made. "When will the island be fully under Roman control?" he asks me once again. He simply has no idea, does he? Why oh why did Titus have to die? Now *there* was an emperor who knew the realities of a military campaign.'

'Domitian needs a victory to shore up his flagging popularity at home,' said Castus. 'He knows that you're the most talented general in the empire, so he's hoping that you'll be the man to deliver it to him.'

'Being talented is not such an advantage in this day and age,' grumbled Agricola. 'Apparently I've attracted the jealousy of Glabrio.'

Lucius's ears pricked up at this mention of the consul's name.

'How do you know?' asked Castus.

'I've received some warnings from friends back in Rome,' muttered the general. 'They say Glabrio is plotting to have me stripped of my command. He's scared that my popularity with the legions will threaten his own power.'

'He can't actually do that, though, can he?'

'He has the ear of the emperor,' said Agricola. 'And that means he probably can – if he sets his mind to it. He has informers everywhere. I would be most surprised if there wasn't one in this camp, waiting for me to say something treasonous which can then be passed on to Domitian. You're not one of Glabrio's informers, are you, Decius?'

'You can trust me with your life, sir, and you know it,' said Castus.

Agricola sighed. 'If only there were more like you, Decius, and fewer like Marcus Acilius Glabrio, the empire would be in a much better state.'

At that moment, with Lucius still eavesdropping, Lurco came surging into the corridor behind him. Lucius flinched and stepped quickly away from the curtain.

'Spying on the general, were you?' Lurco sneered at him. 'Perhaps you were planning to pass on our secrets to your Caledonian friends. The punishment for treachery is death, you know.'

'I–I wasn't spying,' stammered Lucius.

Lurco gave him a sceptical glare. 'So, I hear you've decided to tell all.'

'Yes,' said Quin.

'Well? Let's hear it, then. Where's the enemy camp?'

'We'd rather speak to the general directly, sir,' said Quin.

Lurco's high forehead went pink with indignation. 'You will tell me everything you know this minute, boy, or I'll have you beaten to death!'

'Then you'll be none the wiser,' smiled Quin.

Lurco looked about to strike him across the face for this insolence when the curtain was suddenly swept aside and the camp prefect emerged. The military tribune turned his striking hand into a salute, remaining in this position until Decius Castus had left the praetorium.

'Back already?' said Agricola, eyeing Lucius and Quintus from the tablinum entrance.

Lurco gritted his teeth as he said: 'The Galerii boys have decided to confess the truth about their little adventure.'

'That is good news,' nodded Agricola. 'You see, Tribune Lurco, torture is overrated as a method of extracting information. There's nothing like the prospect of barley rations to get people talking… Come in, you two.' He stood aside to let Lucius and Quin re-enter the tablinum. Lurco was about to follow, but Agricola stopped him.

'That will be all, Tribune, thank you.'

'Are you sure, sir?' said Lurco, inclining his head obsequiously. 'My presence may be valuable to you.'

'I'll summon you if I need you,' said Agricola.

Lurco departed with a barely concealed scowl.

'So,' began the general after taking a seat in one of the hemp-cloth chairs, 'where were you taken?'

Quin swallowed. He cleared his throat, and opened his mouth. But before he could say anything, Lucius jumped in.

'Our name is not Galerius,' he said. He sensed his brother paling with shock at these words, but he forced himself to go on. It was a massive gamble, but after overhearing Agricola's conversation just now, he'd decided that honesty might just be their best hope. 'I am Lucius Valerius Aquila, and this is Quintus

Valerius Felix. Our father was Quintus Valerius Aquila, the senator.'

'I knew him slightly,' said Agricola. 'He was a good man, sadly missed. But why are you telling me this? And if you really are his sons, what in the name of Mithras* are you doing out here play-acting as legionaries?'

Lucius glanced at the two guards standing by the entrance. Mindful of what Agricola had said earlier about Glabrio having spies in the camp, he said: 'Do you mind if we speak with you alone, sir?'

The general looked doubtful.

'We have information that could be of great value to you,' urged Lucius. Agricola seemed to come to a decision. He turned to the guards. 'Search them for weapons,' he said.

As Lucius and Quin endured a rough frisking by the guards, Agricola explained: 'Precautions, you understand.'

The guards pronounced themselves satisfied that neither boy had weapons, and Agricola dismissed them.

When they were alone, Lucius said, without preamble: 'Consul Glabrio killed our father. He killed him because he was about to reveal that Glabrio had murdered the emperor Titus.'

Agricola stood up with such suddenness that

---

* *Mithras: a god of Persian origin who was worshipped in many parts of the Roman empire, including Britannia.*

he knocked his chair over. 'This is monstrous,' he declared. 'Titus died of a fever. He wasn't murdered.'

'That was the story they put out,' said Lucius. 'But my father knew different...' He proceeded to tell Agricola the whole saga of the previous eight months – of what his father and Senator Canio had discovered at the emperor's villa, and how both had paid for that knowledge with their lives, and then how he and Quin had been forced to flee Rome and adopt false identities in order to evade Glabrio's assassins. As he had hoped, Agricola was hooked by the story. He listened with total concentration to every word Lucius spoke, and when a slave arrived to offer the general a cup of wine, he waved him away.

'You've taken a risk in telling me all this,' Agricola interjected when Lucius paused for breath. 'How do you know I'm not an ally of Glabrio's?'

Lucius looked sheepish. 'I'm sorry to say I overheard some of your conversation with the camp prefect just now.'

Agricola didn't smile – his permanently downturned mouth appeared incapable of such an expression – but Lucius discerned a twinkle in his eye, and was suddenly a lot less scared.

Quin, however, simply looked confused.

'Then you obviously realise,' said the general, 'that Glabrio and I are not the best of friends.'

Now Quin began to relax, and a warm grin began to seep across his face.

'I dared to hope that we might have a common interest, sir,' said Lucius.

'You're certainly right about that,' said Agricola. 'In fact, I'd give a great deal to see that man destroyed… But why did you decide to come here, of all places? You couldn't possibly have known about my hatred of Glabrio before you set out. And if your purpose was simply to hide, I can think of few less hospitable places in the empire.'

Quin took over the story at this point. 'It all began,' he said, 'with the discovery of a dead body in the Tiber…' He told Agricola about the physician Diomedes and the autopsy report, and how Parmenion, who had been entrusted with it, had joined up with the Twentieth Legion.

'Parmenion?' said Agricola when Quin mentioned the name. 'You mean the young immunis who's been serving as my scribe these past few weeks?'

'Yes, that would be him!' cried Lucius. 'He was recommended by Manius Julianus Demetrius, a former centurion of this legion.'

Agricola nodded. 'That's the man… But I had no idea he worked for Diomedes. Parmenion probably thought it wisest not to mention his connection to the late doctor…'

'Is he here?' asked Lucius.

'No,' said Agricola vaguely as he tried to absorb all that he'd heard. 'The young man took ill. So I gave him leave to go and get himself better.'

'Where did he go?' asked Quin.

'He told me he was heading for a small settlement in the southwest of Britannia built around a hot spring. Aquae Sulis,* it's called. The mineral waters there are famed for their healing powers.' Agricola's forehead creased in thought. 'Funny thing was, he begged me not to tell a soul that he'd gone there – so I haven't... until now. Poor chap looked scared as well as sick.'

'Scared?' said Lucius, alarmed.

All three appeared to have been struck by the same thought.

'Parmenion didn't just go to Aquae Sulis to get cured,' said Quin, '– he also went there to escape from his murderer.'

Agricola nodded. 'It never occurred to me until this moment, but now I think about it, he had that look about him, as if he'd been poisoned... I've long suspected that Glabrio has spies in this camp. Someone must have worked out the connection between Parmenion and Diomedes, and that Parmenion might have this autopsy report with him.'

'Lurco!' Lucius and Quin blurted out the name simultaneously.

'Excuse me?' queried Agricola.

'Your military tribune is most definitely Glabrio's spy,' said Quin, banging his fist on the table.

Lucius elaborated: 'When we asked after Parmenion earlier this evening, Lurco became very suspicious. He

* *Aquae Sulis: present-day Bath, Somerset.*

wanted to know how we knew him. He also mentioned that Parmenion used to be Diomedes's scribe.'

When he heard this, Agricola immediately strode to the arched entrance and swept aside the curtain. 'Where is Tribune Lurco?' he asked one of the guards in the corridor.

'He was here until just a moment ago, sir,' the guard replied. 'He had his, er... ear to the curtain. Then he departed rather quickly.'

'Go at once to the optio statorum,'* Agricola ordered. 'Get him out of bed if necessary. Tell him to arrest Tribune Lurco and bring him here. Hurry!'

'Yes, sir!' The guard raced away.

They waited in tense silence for the guard to return with Lurco.

'Is Aquae Sulis far, sir?' Lucius asked at one point.

'It's well over 450 miles** from here,' said Agricola distractedly. 'About ten days' travel. We can't even be sure he made it there.' He began to pace the floor. 'By Minerva! What is keeping them?'

Eventually the optio statorum appeared, his grey hair mussed from having recently been roused from his bed. Lurco was not with him. The optio, a plump, craggy-faced, broken-nosed man by the name of Vibius Falco, reported that the military tribune was not in his quarters, and was in fact no longer on the base. 'I've just questioned the sentries at the gate, sir,'

* optio statorum: officer in charge of camp security.

** 450 (Roman) miles: about 670 kilometres.

he said, 'and they told me that Tribune Lurco, together with four other men, left Pinnata on horseback some twenty minutes ago.'

Agricola cursed under his breath.

'He must have heard you tell us where Parmenion had gone,' said Lucius.

'And that's where he and his friends are heading,' muttered Quin.

'Then you must get after them,' Agricola said to Falco. 'Take a cavalry detachment if you have to.' He went over to the wall map, and used his sword to indicate a southward route along the western side of the island. 'They'll be heading this way, going through Luguvalium, Mancunium, Viroconium and Glevum,[*] aiming ultimately for Aquae Sulis.' He prodded a small red dot just east of Portus Abonae on the coast of a large estuary.[**] 'I'm counting on you to intercept them before they get there. There's a man in Aquae Sulis by the name of Parmenion. You may recall him. He's my former scribe. Lurco and his henchmen are going to try and kill him. They're also going to try and steal something very valuable from him – a document upon which the entire future safety of this empire rests. Your job is to stop them from doing that – and bring the document back to me.'

'How will I know what this document looks like?'

---

[*] *Luguvalium: Carlisle; Mancunium: Manchester; Viroconium: Wroxeter; Glevum: Gloucester.*

[**] *Portus Abonae: Sea Mills, now a suburb of Bristol, on the Severn Estuary.*

the optio asked.

Before Agricola could reply, Quin broke in. 'Sir, if you could give my brother and me leave to accompany the optio, we'll help him identify the document.'

Agricola nodded. 'Very well. Help yourselves to whatever supplies and equipment you need. It's vital you catch Lurco and his accomplices before they reach Aquae Sulis.' Agricola removed a ring from his finger. 'This is my official seal,' he said. 'It means you can act in my name – so use it responsibly. It will also allow you to use the cursus publicus,* which should shorten your journey to just three or four days.' He hesitated in the act of handing it to Quin. 'You still haven't told me where the Caledonians took you,' he reminded him. 'If you won't tell me the truth about that, how can I trust you with *this*?'

Quin flashed a desperate glance at Lucius. They both knew there would be no time for their peace mission – not if they wanted to catch Lurco.

Lucius faced Agricola. 'We told you the truth earlier, sir,' he said. 'We escaped before we reached any settlement.'

The general frowned. 'I still think you're concealing something from me, but I don't have time to force it out of you now. This new undertaking is too important.' He handed the ring to Quin. 'When you find the

* *cursus publicus: the official courier and transport service of the Roman empire, used to transport messages, officials and tax revenues. It included a network of mansiones (inns for people on official business) and mutationes (way-stations for changing horses).*

document,' he said, 'don't bring it back here. That will only waste more time, and I suspect that Glabrio will move against me very soon. Take it straight to Rome. I have a powerful friend there by the name of Aulus Pomponius Licinius, who will help you. I'll write to him now and warn him to expect you. Licinius is a senator with lots of experience in the law courts, and one of the few senior figures in Rome who are prepared to speak out against Glabrio. He'll know exactly what to do.'

He ushered the three of them out of the door. 'Now go. Get yourselves to the south! Be quick as Mercury – and ruthless as Mars!'*

* *Mercury: the messenger of the gods; Mars: the god of war.*

PART THREE

SOUTHERN BRITANNIA

CHAPTER XI

18 APRIL

Half an hour later, Lucius, Quin and Falco set out from the camp on the fastest horses the camp's stablemaster could spare. Falco had wanted to take half a dozen of his regular companions on the mission, but Quin soon talked him out of it. 'Stealth is our best weapon,' he argued. 'We don't want them to know they're being followed, so the fewer of us there are on their tail, the better.'

'But there are five of them and only three of us,' Falco had pointed out.

'Quin is worth three of any man,' Lucius assured him.

Reluctantly, Falco had agreed.

They rode southwest through the night, guided by the stars, their way lit by the moon. They galloped across hills and moorland, and negotiated dense forests, bogs and fast-flowing streams. The roads were, for the most part, no better than rough tracks. Every fifteen to twenty miles* they would arrive at a Roman fort where they could change their horses and so maintain their speed. At every stop they asked the garrison commander whether Lurco and his companions had passed this way recently. In each case they were told that they had, thus reassuring the pursuers that they were on the right track. At the first fort they came to, they learned that they were an hour behind their quarry. At the next, they had closed the gap to 'a little less than an hour'. At the next, they were 'about three-quarters of an hour' behind them. This pattern continued, and with each stop they felt themselves drawing closer to the renegade tribune and his cronies.

An hour or so after daybreak, they reached the fortress of Luguvalium – their eighth stop – and were told that Lurco and his men had departed less than a quarter of an hour ago. Encouraged by this news, Quin, Lucius and Falco gobbled down some breakfast, spurred their fresh mounts and galloped south. The road was now much more like the ones Lucius and Quin were used to from Italy – eight paces wide with a smooth, metalled surface, it stretched ahead of them,

* *fifteen to twenty miles: 22–30 kilometres.*

almost ruler-straight, for as far as the eye could see. They almost fancied they could discern a cloud of dust in the distance, thrown up by the hooves of those they were pursuing.

From this point on, the advantages of the cursus publicus became clear, and their journey time would inevitably speed up. Roughly every four miles* – the furthest a horse could safely be ridden hard – they would come to a mutatio, a set of stables where those on official business could change their horses and slake their thirst at a tavern. And every twelve miles, they would reach either a fort or a mansio – a roadside inn with large stables, a tavern, rooms for the night and, in some cases, a bathhouse. The problem was that Lurco, being a military tribune, would be able to avail himself of exactly the same services.

At the first mutatio they came to they were informed that Lurco and his band had 'only just left', so without even stopping for a drink, the trio mounted their new horses and took off. They were tired now – the lack of sleep catching up with them – but they forced themselves on, knowing how close they were to their target. Three miles later, they caught their first glimpse of Lurco and his fellow horsemen riding at full gallop up a hill towards the fort of Voreda.** Lucius whipped his horse faster as he saw the fort gates open to admit Lurco and his friends.

* *four miles: 6 kilometres.*

** *Voreda: Penrith, Cumbria.*

'We've got them like flies trapped in a jar!' yelled Quin triumphantly as they charged along.

When they reached the gates, Falco bellowed in a voice that Centurion Gallicus would have been proud of: 'By order of Proconsul Gnaeus Julius Agricola, open these gates!'

The gates were duly opened, and Falco, followed by Lucius and Quin, trotted into the main courtyard of the small fort. The place was dotted with garrison troops, but there was no sign of Lurco or his men.

'Send for the garrison commander,' Falco demanded of the sentry, as the three of them dismounted.

A red-faced, flustered-looking centurion appeared before them a few minutes later.

'Are you in command here?' asked Falco.

'I am deputy,' said the centurion. 'Commander is currently, er, sick.' His Latin was halting, foreign-accented.

'Five men arrived here just a few minutes ago,' said Falco. 'One of them is the military tribune Appius Mallius Lurco. We're under orders from General Agricola to arrest these men for treason.' He showed the man Agricola's seal ring with its gemstone carved with the general's profile. 'Please bring them to me at once.'

The man didn't move. 'We have not seen these men,' he said.

'Liar!' roared Falco. 'We saw them enter this fort not five minutes ago.'

'You are mistaking them for other men, I think,' said the deputy commander with a defiant jut of his lower lip.

Lucius wondered what reason the man could have for lying. The people they had seen entering the fort could only have been Lurco and his men. Something was wrong. Where was the commander? Lucius scanned the ragtag crew of garrison troops watching them from the walls and barrack-room doorways. He observed their slack, unshaven faces, long hair and lazy stares. These were auxiliaries – from Gaul,* most likely, to judge from the accent of their deputy commander – and nothing like the highly disciplined legionaries he'd seen back at Pinnata. Their loyalty to Rome had to be bought – they were little better than mercenaries in that sense. It made him feel uneasy – vulnerable almost – to be surrounded by these armed strangers.

Falco had lost patience. He drew his sword and held it to the deputy's throat. 'Bring those men to me now,' he hissed, 'or I'll slit your throat in front of your troops.'

Suddenly, a sound ripped through the air – a whine followed by a thump. Lucius stared in disbelief as Falco's knees buckled beneath him and he slumped to the ground, sword and seal ring tumbling from his hand. A metal bolt protruded from his chest. It had

---

* *Gaul: the Roman name for a large area of Europe, consisting of modern France and parts of neighbouring countries.*

smashed right through his breastplate.

'Down!' screamed Quin, and both he and Lucius threw themselves to the ground, just as another iron bolt flew close above their heads.

Lucius scrambled after his brother on his hands and knees, as they both made for the shelter of the fort's gatehouse. There came another click and whistle, and Lucius felt a terrible scorching on the back of his neck. He fell flat to the ground and clasped his hand over the wound, screwing up his eyes against the agony. Quin grabbed him by the crook of his shoulder and dragged him behind the gate. Removing his hand, Lucius saw blood, but not much. The burn was ferociously painful, though.

'You'll live,' said Quin, glancing at the wound. 'It's just a scrape, don't worry.'

'What's happening?' gasped Lucius.

Quin risked a peek into the courtyard. 'It's one of Lurco's cronies,' he said. 'I can see his outline at the window of the praetorium.'

Lucius, peering over his shoulder, saw that the courtyard was now almost deserted – the troops had made themselves scarce as soon as the bolts had started flying – apart from the deputy, who stood in the middle of the open space, rigid with fear.

'He must have got hold of a cheiroballistra,' said Quin.

'What's that?' asked Lucius, still wincing from the pain coursing through his neck.

'It's a kind of spring-loaded bow and arrow. Very powerful. Hunters use them. Didn't know it could penetrate armour, though. Poor Falco!'

Quin ducked back out of sight. 'One of Lurco's men has just come outside. He's heading over to Falco's body.'

'What's he doing?' asked Lucius.

'No idea...' Then Quin smashed his fist in the dust. 'Curses! He's going to steal Agricola's seal ring, isn't he? They know we'll be powerless to stop them without that.' He glanced once more into the courtyard, then rose to his feet. 'I'll have to risk it,' he said, gritting his teeth. 'I'll have to go out there and stop him.'

But Lucius pulled him back. 'You can't,' he said. 'You'll be killed by that... cheiro-thingy as soon as you step out there.'

Then Lucius had an idea. Removing the pugio* from his belt, he slipped in front of Quin so he could get his own view of the courtyard.

Lurco's man had just scooped up the ring from the ground and was now turning back towards the praetorium. He was about twelve paces from the gate – this would be the furthest throw Lucius had ever attempted. And there was no time to prepare himself – when the man started running, the distance between them would rapidly increase and hitting him would become virtually impossible. Lucius took aim, at the same time trying to work out the kind of

* *pugio: dagger.*

force and trajectory he would need to cover such a distance. Then he leaned back, twisting his shoulder and pushing his throwing hand behind his head. He steadied his breathing, counted to three, and let fly, just as the man began to run. The dagger arced across the courtyard, its blade catching the sunlight in flashes as it tumbled.

The throw was good… and it landed square in the middle of the running man's back.

He tumbled with a groan, spilling the ring.

'You genius!' yelled Quin gleefully. 'You absolute genius!'

This second death jolted the deputy into panicked life. He started gabbling in his native language and running towards Lucius at the gate, his eyes wide with terror. The man was shaking his head and his hands wildly – he seemed to be begging Lucius and Quin either to give themselves up or to escape. His hysteria was interrupted by another click-whistle-thud. He stopped running, his screams turned to chokes, and he keeled over face down, an iron bolt in his back.

Lucius never found out whether the cheiroballistra had been aimed at the deputy commander or himself. But the death of the deputy, whether deliberate or not, changed everything. The man must have been popular with his men, because when they saw him fall, the previously lethargic auxiliaries immediately came rushing out of their barrack blocks and charged en masse towards the praetorium. One or two may have been killed by iron bolts during the charge, but this deterred no one. Lucius and Quin could only watch as the troops trampled over the man Lucius had downed with his knife, and swarmed through the praetorium entrance in a killing frenzy. Within minutes, three blood-soaked corpses were carried out into the courtyard and dumped unceremoniously on the ground next to the one already there. None of them looked like Lurco.

A minute or so later, a battered and bruised garrison commander emerged from the praetorium and began issuing instructions to his troops, trying to re-establish order on the base. Lucius and Quin returned to the courtyard. Lucius retrieved the seal ring and his pugio, while Quin went in search of Lurco. He was dismayed to discover that the man had vanished.

'The one you are looking for is gone,' the commander confirmed as he dabbed blood from his face with a damp cloth. 'He stole one of our horses during all the confusion just now… We are sorry for this mess, and sorry for the death of your companion. As soon as those men arrived here, they took me hostage and forced my deputy to lie to you.' The commander eyed the bodies of four of his erstwhile captors. 'I hope you find the fifth one and kill him,' he said angrily. 'You must avenge the death of my deputy.'

CHAPTER XII

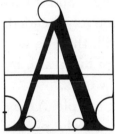fter resting for a few hours at Voreda, Lucius and Quin raced south. They stopped at every fort, town, mansio and mutatio, asking each time if Lurco had passed that way, and were always greeted with the same answer: no, he hadn't. Not a single person they spoke to had seen the military tribune. They could only conclude that he had chosen an alternative route to Aquae Sulis in an attempt to evade them. This was good news in one sense, for they were confident that theirs was the most direct route to the town, so they were bound to reach Parmenion before him. But it was also bad news, because they now had no idea where Lurco was or what he might be planning.

On the morning of their fourth day on the road, they reached the settlement of Aquae Sulis. The small town nestled on the banks of a meandering river known in the local tongue as the Abona.* Within its walls they found a ferment of activity. Its few streets were filled with people of different skin tones and accents, sampling food from takeaway stalls, or buying healing potions or effigies of the town's patron goddess, Sulis-Minerva. Aquae Sulis seemed to be a thriving, expanding settlement, with at least a dozen new buildings under construction at its edges. At the centre of the town lay the sole reason for its success – a stone temple housing a sacred spring – and it was to here that Lucius and Quin instinctively headed. They reasoned that if Parmenion was ill, then he was likely to spend his days trying to restore his health by bathing in the spring's famous healing waters.

The crowds were thickest outside the temple. A long line of sickly, limping, maimed and elderly people queued before the entrance. Quin flashed Agricola's seal at the official at the head of the queue. The official pushed aside a couple of lame beggars so that Quin and Lucius could pass through. They mounted the staircase, passed between the pillars and entered the cella of the temple. The cella was dominated by a large bronze statue of the goddess, where a few people

---

* Abona: the word for 'river' in the Brittonic or Brythonic language (the ancestor of modern Welsh, Cornish and Breton). The modern name Avon derives from this, so 'River Avon' literally means 'River River'.

were kneeling or laying their votive gifts. However, most worshippers passed straight through the temple and out into the adjoining courtyard.

A small, elderly man with a high, domed forehead approached them as they entered. He was dressed in the robes of a sacerdos, or temple priest. He greeted a young man standing next to them, who nodded and twitched a great deal before hobbling out into the courtyard. The sacerdos then turned his attention to Lucius and Quin.

'Welcome to the temple of the goddess Sulis-Minerva,' he said to them with a small bow. 'We are not generally honoured by the presence of legionaries, unless they've been wounded in battle. Are you seeking a tour of the temple and its grounds? I can tell you that it was built nearly forty years ago, shortly after the occupation. The natural hot spring, which you will find in the courtyard, has been a place of worship for the native people of this area since time immemorial. They call the goddess of the spring Sulis, hence the name of the town, 'Waters of Sulis'. We believe that Sulis is actually a manifestation of Minerva, goddess of wisdom, and are strongly encouraging the locals to worship her by her new name, Sulis-Minerva. Now, if you'll follow me into the courtyard, I can show you –'

'Thank you, Sacerdos,' interrupted Quin, 'but we're not tourists. We actually need your help on an official matter. May we go somewhere more private?' He showed the priest the seal ring.

The sacerdos stared at it for a moment, before nodding. 'Of course,' he said. 'Please come this way.' He led them into a small, cluttered annex towards the rear of the temple, which served as a private office. He seated himself at a desk piled high with thin lead tablets. Lucius recognised them as defixiones – curse tablets.

'You wouldn't believe how many of these get flung into the sacred spring each week,' said the priest, observing Lucius's interest. 'Some are left around the edges of the spring and I must remove them from time to time as they do clutter up the place. It's also interesting for me to read what people are saying and who they are cursing. Keeps me in touch with the concerns of the community, you understand… Now, how may I be of service?'

'We're trying to locate a certain individual,' said Quin. 'His name is Parmenion.'

This seemed to surprise the sacerdos. 'How strange,' he said. 'You're the second person to ask me about Parmenion this morning…'

Lucius and Quin stared at each other in shock.

Lurco! But how?

'…and I'll say to you exactly what I said to the first man,' continued the priest. 'I've never heard of anyone by that name.'

'Wh–who was this other person?' stammered Lucius.

'I'm afraid he swore me to secrecy.'

'Remember who you're speaking to,' said Quin gently but firmly. 'We're agents of the proconsul.'

'Oh, this man also showed me a fancy seal,' said the sacerdos. 'Claimed he was a military tribune or something. So who am I supposed to believe?'

'It *was* Tribune Lurco, then!' exclaimed Quin. 'By Mercury, how could he have got here before us?'

'You know him, then,' said the sacerdos, before clamping a hand over his mouth. 'Whoops! Gave the game away there, didn't I? Well, I suppose your seal trumps his – and, in any case, I wasn't completely sure if he really was a military tribune...'

'Why's that?'

'To look at him, one had to have one's doubts. He was unshaven, his uniform was filthy and he was caked in dust.'

'So that's how he did it,' said Lucius. 'He must have slept rough by the roadside each night.' It almost made him smile to think of the haughty and effete Lurco forced to sleep in the open, exposed to all that inclement Britannic weather.

Quin nodded, then turned back to the sacerdos. 'Where is Lurco now?'

'Well, he insisted on searching the temple, the courtyard and the sacred spring, and when he couldn't find this Parmenion fellow anywhere, he went off into the town to look for him there.'

Lucius was bitterly disappointed that the priest hadn't heard of Parmenion – and now also worried that Lurco was one step ahead of them in the hunt.

'Thank you for your help, sacerdos,' said Quin, as he and Lucius headed for the door.

'Good luck with your search,' said the sacerdos, switching his attention to the lead tablets on his desk. The brothers were on their way out when he suddenly shouted: 'Wait just a minute!'

They turned to see him staring at one of the tablets. 'This tribune you were talking about,' he said. 'What's his full name?'

'Appius Mallius Lurco,' said Lucius.

The sacerdos held up the tablet in his hand so Lucius could see it. 'Look at the words on this one,' he said.

Lucius and Quin looked at it:

OH DIVINE SULIS, I CALL UPON THEE FOR DIVINE
RETRIBUTION AGAINST APPIUS MALLIUS LURCO,
WHO HAS POISONED MY BLOOD AND STOLEN
MY HEALTH AND YOUTH. DO NOT ALLOW SLEEP
TO THIS MAN. CURSE HIS BLOOD, HIS EYES,
HIS EVERY LIMB.

'What kind of a language is that?' puzzled Quin.

'It's Latin,' said the sacerdos, 'but it's been reversed. Curse writers often do that – they believe it adds power to the malediction. I apologise – I forgot that not everyone is accustomed to reading mirror writing.' He rummaged around in a trunk in the corner filled with bronze and pottery ritual vessels until he found a polished bronze platter, which he held up to the tablet. 'Can you read it now?'

The brothers peered at the reflected words:

OH DIVINE SULIS, I CALL UPON THEE FOR DIVINE
RETRIBUTION AGAINST APPIUS MALLIUS LURCO,
WHO HAS POISONED MY BLOOD AND STOLEN
MY HEALTH AND YOUTH. DO NOT ALLOW SLEEP
TO THIS MAN. CURSE HIS BLOOD, HIS EYES,
HIS EVERY LIMB.

Lucius clenched his fists in excitement when he read this. It could only have been written by Parmenion!

'This proves he's been here!' said Quin.

'What's more, I recognise the script,' said the sacerdos. 'See how fine it is. The man is clearly a professional scribe. And the Latin is faultless, unlike the vulgar forms of our language that I so often encounter on these defixiones. I have conversed a few times with the man who wrote this. He goes by the name of Socrates. The poor fellow is in a very sickly state. Now I think of it, I remember him mentioning that he believed he'd been poisoned.'

'He must be using a false name for his own protection,' said Lucius.

'Do you have any idea where he is?' asked Quin.

'He's here. You'll find him at the sacred spring in the courtyard. In fact, he was the man I greeted just before I spoke to you.'

Lucius couldn't believe they'd been standing just a few feet from the man they'd been searching for all this time. He and Quin immediately jumped up and raced out of the office with barely even a thank-you and farewell for the sacerdos. They hurtled through the cella and out through a side exit into the courtyard. Lucius prayed that Parmenion hadn't departed while they'd been talking to the sacerdos.

The courtyard was a wide, rectangular space bordered on three sides by high stone walls. In the centre was a huge altar stone, as tall as a man, its upper surface covered in the ashes of a recent sacrifice. But the focus of everyone's attention was not on this – it was on a tall, brick-built, barrel-vaulted structure in the left-hand corner of the courtyard. Steam poured through its arched entrance, reminding Lucius of one of Vulcan's[*] fire-breathing bronze bulls. The long queue of worshippers standing before its mouth seemed almost like sacrificial victims.

'That's got to be the sacred spring,' said Lucius. He scanned the line of people, trying to recall how the sickly young man had looked. He had been very thin, he remembered, with hair cut close to his scalp, and his body had been full of involuntary twitches. He couldn't see anyone like that in the courtyard. 'Parmenion must be inside,' he told Quin.

They jostled their way to the front of the queue.

---

[*] *Vulcan: god of fire, metalwork and various handicrafts. He was able to make animated statues, including a pair of fire-breathing bulls.*

A few glared at them, but no one complained: their swords and legionary uniforms gave them an automatic status that no one dared question.

Eventually, they stood before a burly-looking temple official at the steamy mouth of the building. His job was to restrict the number of people admitted at any one time, so the sacred spring did not become too crowded. Quin showed him the seal ring. After frowning at it for a moment, the official stood aside to let them enter.

At first they could see nothing through the swirling, ghostly clouds of steam. Gradually, as they moved forward, the interior revealed itself, the gleaming brick walls and arched roof slick with moisture and green slime. Shafts of light, shooting through the barred, arched window at the far end, brightened the wet, steamy air. And below them, at the bottom of a few slippery steps, lay a large, oval pool filled with bubbling green water, set within a red-tiled floor. This was the sacred spring – a magical, never-ending source of hot water surging up from the bowels of the earth. Lucius could tell at once why the Britons, and now the Romans, who came here believed they were entering the presence of a goddess. Rising out of the mist-covered water were columns and statues of water nymphs. He could also discern figures of people kneeling by the pool, splashing it over their bodies and praying.

Lucius felt hot in his armour. Sweat broke out

on his face, and within seconds his tunic was damp. Squinting through the foggy air, he spotted the thin, twitching figure of Parmenion near the far end of the pool, seated cross-legged on the edge of the surround.

'Over there,' he said to Quin.

They walked carefully down the steps and made their way around the pool. Parmenion shrank from them in flinching terror as they approached, his mouth widening into a dark hole as if he was about to scream. His skull-like face seemed at that moment nothing but mouth and eyes.

Lucius crouched next to him and placed a reassuring hand on his shoulder. 'It's all right,' he said. 'Don't be scared. We don't want to hurt you. We're your friends.'

'You're L–Lurco's men, aren't you?' stammered Parmenion. 'You've come to f–f–finish me off!'

Lucius shook his head. 'We're here to stop Lurco,' he said, 'and to make sure you're safe.'

Parmenion stared at him with huge, frightened eyes. He wiped drool from his mouth. 'Look at me,' he whined, grabbing a piece of his scrawny upper arm. 'I'm almost dead. That man's poison's done its work. Hemlock! The same plant that did for Socrates* – that's why I took his name. Lurco put it in my food... You can't save me now. No one can.'

'We can and we will,' said Lucius.

The scribe gave a violent twitch, then seemed to

---

* Socrates: a famous Greek philosopher of the 5th century BC. He was condemned to die by drinking poison made from the hemlock plant.

relax. 'Wh–who are you if you're not Lurco's men?' he asked. 'Why are you here?'

'We met with your mistress Claudia back in Rome,' said Lucius. 'She told us about the autopsy report, and how you brought it here with you. We want to use it to bring down Glabrio. He killed our father, so we have a personal reason to destroy him.'

Parmenion looked more closely at Lucius. 'You're Caecilia's boy, aren't you?'

Lucius almost fell backwards in surprise. 'How do you know?'

'I met her a few times,' he said. 'You look a lot like her.'

'Well, then you must know I'm telling the truth,' said Lucius. 'Our father, her husband, was Quintus Valerius Aquila.'

'I know,' said Parmenion. His head jerked as he said this, and another string of saliva fell from his lower lip.

In the hot, misty gloom, figures moved around them. New people arrived as others departed.

'Do you have the autopsy report?' asked Quin.

Parmenion stared up at him. 'Yes,' he said. 'Not here with me, but it's safe. I also have a signed affidavit from Diomedes stating that Glabrio forced him to change the report. The two documents together, in the right hands, should be enough to finish off that monster.'

Hearing this, Lucius felt a surge of hope. 'Where are they?' he asked, unable to keep the excitement out of his voice.

'They're in a chest of my personal papers in Londinium.'*

'Londinium?' cried Quin. 'Why in Hades are they there?'

Despite the heat, Lucius felt the bitter chill of disappointment. Just as they had seemed within touching distance of their goal, yet another journey loomed. Londinium was the province's main port and biggest city – and it lay a hundred miles** to the east.

'I didn't want to risk taking the papers north with me,' explained Parmenion, 'so I left them in the hands of a trusted friend. His name is Vibius Favonius Felix and he runs the gladiator school in Londinium. I told him I'd come back one day to reclaim the papers, but...' Parmenion's body made an involuntary shudder. He looked pale and wretched. '...I don't think that's going to happen, do you?' He eyed Lucius. 'You, my friend, and your brother – I must count on you two to retrieve the report and bring Glabrio to justice. Here, let me write something for you...' Weakly, he reached behind him for one of the thin lead tablets people used to write their curses on. Taking up a stylus, he began scratching words into the metal surface. He wrote at speed, yet his script was impressively regular, with each letter beautifully formed – except once when the poison in his system made his body convulse, causing the pen to fly off in the wrong direction. 'Curses on

* *Londinium: London.*

** *a hundred (Roman) miles: about 150 kilometres.*

you, Lurco,' Parmenion murmured, before continuing with the letter. When it was finished, he rolled it up tightly and handed it to Lucius. 'Show this to Felix when you see him and he'll know that you come with my blessing,' he said.

'Come with us,' Lucius said to Parmenion, holding out his hand to him. 'Lurco is in town. If you stay here, he'll find you.'

Parmenion's breathing became shallower and more spasmodic. 'Lurco is here?'

'If you come with us now, we'll keep you safe,' Lucius promised.

Parmenion appeared to grow calmer as he considered this. Finally, he looked up at Lucius. 'No,' he said. 'I'll only slow you down, and it's vital that you get hold of those documents. That's far more important than my life. Lurco's as good as killed me already – what does it matter if he finishes me off a little sooner?'

'Are you sure?' asked Lucius. He felt sorry for the young man, and disturbed by his fatalism.

'I've never been more certain about anything,' said Parmenion, and he seemed to fade a little behind a cloud of steam, as if the goddess had already begun to steal him away from them. Lucius guessed that Parmenion planned to die here in her sanctuary.

He felt Quin's hand on his arm. 'We'd better go,' said Quin. But Lucius hesitated. There was something that Parmenion had said earlier that was nagging at him. He had to ask him about it – there would never be another chance.

'You said you met my mother a few times,' said Lucius. 'As far as I know, my family never moved in the same circles as Diomedes. So where did you meet her?'

Parmenion stared sorrowfully at his reflection in the bubbling green water. 'You don't want to know, my friend,' he said.

'Please!' begged Lucius.

Parmenion remained silent for a while. Finally, he looked up at Lucius. 'My master, Diomedes, was also physician to Glabrio,' he said. 'He and I occasionally visited the consul at his home. Sometimes, your mother was there... This was before your father died.'

The sweat on Lucius's back turned to ice. He recalled his mother's whispered prayer to Venus in the temple back in Rome, asking her to bless her forthcoming marriage to Glabrio. That had been hard enough to swallow. But he'd assumed that their relationship had begun *after* his father's death. Was it possible that it had begun *before*?

'Are you saying my mother was more than a friend to Glabrio – while she was still married to my father?'

'I'm afraid so, yes,' said Parmenion. 'And there's worse...'

Lucius felt as though he might faint. The heat was becoming oppressive. Part of him wanted to escape this steaming, claustrophobic chamber, and the words that he knew would hurt him – yet a stronger part kept him rooted to the spot. He had to know the truth, however terrible.

Parmenion was looking increasingly like a ghost as the mist wreathed his pale, thin body. He continued with his story: 'One evening in early September last year, the master and I were visiting Glabrio, who was suffering from a nervous disorder. Before we were admitted to the consul's chamber, my master had to visit the kitchen to request the preparation of a decoction. I remained waiting outside the chamber, and while I was standing there I overheard Glabrio speaking with your mother. They said many things to each other, but during the course of the conversation I distinctly heard him say the words 'Titus' and 'sea-hare' and 'poison'. I thought nothing of it at the time. But then, a few days later, the emperor died, and my master wrote his report. Only then did I put the pieces together.'

'Are you really saying our mother knew about the murder of the emperor before it took place?' demanded Quin.

'I'm only telling you what I heard,' answered the scribe.

'Come on!' Quin said to Lucius. 'I've heard enough of this rubbish.'

But Lucius couldn't move. He remembered how angry Caecilia had been with their father when he warned them he would expose the murderer. But could she really have been part of the plot to kill Titus? If that was true, then their quest to bring down Glabrio could very well end up killing her as well…

As Quin moved away, a figure who had been sitting crouched over the water beside Parmenion suddenly shifted closer to him. Parmenion screamed. It was a loud and terrible sound, almost like the screech of a bird, and it seemed to echo forever inside the vaulted brick chamber.

Lucius and Quin drew their swords as dark blood poured from Parmenion's side, mingling with the green water of the spring. Parmenion's death scream was quickly blotted out by a cacophony of terrified cries and scampering footsteps as the other worshippers at the spring desperately tried to get away.

Parmenion's body keeled forward and disappeared beneath the boiling water with barely a splash. His killer unbent himself and rose to his feet, the glimmering blade of a gladius extending from his hand. Lucius recognised Lurco's small, shiny face and sneering mouth. He wondered why the tribune should be looking so smug, considering he was outnumbered. Then a clash of steel behind him made Lucius turn, and he saw that Quin had been set upon by a pair of swordsmen – the tribune must have recruited a couple more henchmen. An intuitive sense of danger made Lucius turn back just as Lurco was leaping towards him. Lucius met his blade with his own when it was just a finger's-breadth from his face. Any closer and it could have taken a slice out of his cheek. Using all his strength, he forced Lurco's blade back and tried to kick out with his right foot in an attempt to knock him into the pool. But Lurco jerked out of range. The tribune came at Lucius while he was still off-balance, but his attack was amateurish, and easily rebutted. They began to hack at each other, the clinks of their swords sounding like blacksmiths' hammers in the confined space. In the dim haze of the chamber, with its flickering shafts of sunlight, Lurco appeared only half-solid as he darted in and out of view. Their sandals squeaked on the slimy, narrow shelf of tiles that surrounded the pool, as each tried to manoeuvre the other over the edge and into the scalding water.

There was a splash and a scream from behind. Lucius glanced briefly over his shoulder to see one of Quin's opponents thrashing around in agony in the superheated water. Lurco tried to take advantage of Lucius's distraction with a kick to his leg. Pain blazed in Lucius's shin and, with a wave of hot terror, he realised he was losing balance and about to fall in the water himself. He wheeled his arms in his desperation. By bending forward at the waist, he just managed to grab hold of the opposite wall and rescue himself. While Lucius was still in this position, Lurco tried to drive his sword into his side, but Lucius quickly spun out of the way and then sliced downwards.

Lurco screamed, and Lucius wondered what he'd done. Then he saw the tribune's hand, still gripping the sword, falling to the floor. Lurco fell to his knees, clutching at the bleeding stump of his wrist. Lucius considered finishing him off, but couldn't bring himself to. Instead, he turned to see how Quin was getting on. His brother was wrestling with his remaining opponent. Both were pushing at each other hard with the edges of their swords. The other man then tripped Quin, sending him sprawling onto his stomach. As he landed, something flew out of his hand and plopped into the water.

Agricola's seal ring! Gone!

The man drove his sword towards Quin's head, but before blade could meet flesh, Lucius struck with a thrust of his gladius into the man's side. The man's own sword clattered harmlessly onto the tiles as he fell, lifeless, to the floor.

Silence... apart from the wretched sobbing of Lurco. Lucius ripped a strip off the hem of his tunic, then kneeled down next to Lurco, who had folded himself into a foetal position, crying and clutching at his wound. Gently, Lucius reached for the man's shaking, bleeding stump and began wrapping the fabric around it as tightly as he could.

Behind him, he could hear impatience in Quin's voice as he said: 'Let's leave him. He doesn't deserve our help.' Lucius ignored him and carried on. Lurco groaned in agony, and the improvised bandage was soon dark and wet with fresh blood, but Lucius hoped it would stem the flow well enough until the wound could be cauterised by a surgeon.

He followed Quin out of the sacred spring. The courtyard was deserted. Everyone had fled. Lucius was grateful for the cool, fresh air in his lungs. He closed his eyes and tried to calm himself, but his mind was in turmoil. The nightmarish sounds and sights he'd just experienced would, he knew, haunt him for months, maybe years, to come. That sacred place had become, for Lucius, a den of horror.

CHAPTER XIII

4–5 JUNE

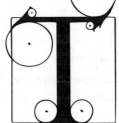hree days later, Lucius and Quin arrived in Londinium. This was not their first visit to the city – they had spent a day and a night there a month ago, during their journey to Caledonia. Now, as Lucius rode through the town alongside his brother, he got the sense once again of a city on the rise. Twenty-two years earlier, Londinium had been burned to the ground by the Iceni tribe, led by their queen Boudica.* Since then it had been rebuilt as a planned Roman town with wide streets, temples, bathhouses, and a forum and basilica** at its centre.

---

* *Boudica (also called Boadicea): a British queen who revolted against Roman rule after the death of her husband, Prasutagus. She destroyed Camulodunum (Colchester) and Verulamium (St Albans) as well as Londinium, but was eventually defeated by the Roman general Suetonius.*

** *basilica: a public building used as a law court and for business meetings.*

Everywhere they looked there was evidence of new construction – but unlike at Aquae Sulis, here they were building in stone, not timber, with tile replacing thatch on the rooftops. Carts laden with blocks of cut stone creaked their way up from the river. Lucius and Quin, on horseback, had to take care to avoid the trenches that had been dug in the cobbled streets to lay water and drainage pipes, and the pits where workmen mixed the mortar. Over the charred remnants of earlier buildings – fading reminders of Queen Boudica's fury – foundations were being laid for new houses, with stacks of cemented clay tiles embedded for underfloor heating systems.* They saw mosaicists at work, and a new street fountain being installed. And on the edge of the city, a stone wall was rising. As Isi had commented during their first visit, it was as though the Romans wanted to make a statement to any rebellious Britons out there: *Whether you like it or not, we're here to stay!*

This, of course, reminded Lucius of Isi. He wondered how she was. He could picture her now, giving lessons to the young Caledonian warriors each day and joining in with the communal singing, eating and storytelling around the campfire each evening. He wondered if she would settle down for good up there in the wild north. Did she ever lie awake at night and think of him, as he so often did of her? Or had she

---

* *underfloor heating systems: floors in wealthy Roman houses were supported on short pillars made of tiles. Hot air from a furnace circulated between the pillars, warming the room. The system was called by the Greek name* hypocaust.

already forgotten him? One day, no doubt, she'd fall in love with a Caledonian boy, and then Lucius and all the adventures they'd shared would fade forever from her mind. This thought was like a stab in his heart.

In the northwest of the city, not far from the legionary fortress, lay a small amphitheatre. Just to the east of this was the ludus – the gladiator training school – where they hoped to find Parmenion's friend, the surgeon Vibius Favonius Felix. It was an anonymous, forbidding structure of high brick walls and small barred windows. The brickwork looked hastily done and was already showing signs of wear and tear. After tethering their horses, Lucius and Quin knocked on the iron-studded oak door. It was opened by a muscular blond man with a curling moustache and frowning eyes. Seeing their uniforms, his face recomposed itself into a slightly less surly expression. 'How can I be of help?' he asked in crude Latin.

'We'd like to see the manager of this ludus, Vibius Favonius Felix,' said Quin.

'This not possible,' the porter answered.

'Now wait a minute,' snapped Quin. 'You can't stop us. We're here on the orders of the proconsul.' Not for the first time, Lucius rued the loss of Agricola's seal ring in the sacred spring of Aquae Sulis. On the way here, it had been enough of a struggle to convince officials at forts and mansiones of their credentials, and on more than one night they'd been forced to sleep rough. Still, Quin was not the type to feel cowed by a recalcitrant porter, and a week of almost non-stop riding had taken its toll on his patience. 'You show us to Felix this instant,' he demanded, 'or I'll see you consigned to an iron mine for the remainder of your sorry life!'

'This not possible,' the porter repeated calmly. 'Favonius Felix – he dead.'

A shudder ran through Lucius when he heard this. *Surely Lurco couldn't be behind this – the severely maimed military tribune must still be recovering from his injury.*

'What do you mean, he's dead?' yelled Quin, who seemed unable to accept this latest setback. He barged past the porter into the vestibule of the ludus. 'You take us to him now!' he demanded.

'What's going on?' boomed a deep voice. Lucius was uncertain at first from where it had emanated. Then he glanced beyond the porter, beyond Quin, to the far end of the vestibule where it led through to an open-air training quadrangle. Standing there, blocking out most of the daylight, was the enormous silhouette of a man.

'What do you want?' bellowed the man, his voice echoing around the stone walls and ceiling like a wildly shaken sistrum.*

Lucius stepped past the porter to join Quin. On closer inspection, the man was not a giant on the scale of Baltair, though he was far uglier. And his voice did not quite hit the decibel level of Centurion Gallicus,

---

* *sistrum: a metal rattle used in some religious ceremonies.*

though the sound was much more grating on the ear. He was bald, and his face was disfigured by a deep scar that ran from chin to ear. But the scar did not disturb Lucius as much as the heavily hooded eyes, which seemed to glitter with sinister intentions.

'We're agents of General Agricola,' said Quin. 'We wish to speak to the manager, Favonius Felix. Is he really dead?'

The big man nodded. 'He's dead all right. Training accident. Three days ago.'

He said this in a flat, metallic voice, his face expressionless except for his eyes, which were filled with vicious contempt.

'What do you mean, "training accident"?' said Quin. 'I understood he ran this school – he wasn't a fighter.'

'He was lanista* as well as manager here,' said the man. 'We were in the practice arena over there.' He jerked a thumb over his shoulder towards a miniature arena at the far end of the quad. 'What can I say? Accidents happen.'

'So you killed him?' said Quin.

'I suppose I did. In a manner of speaking.'

'And who runs the place now?'

'You're looking at him.'

'You're the new manager and lanista of the school?'

The man spat some yellow phlegm onto the floor tiles. 'The name's Clodius Juba.'

Quin smiled and nodded. 'Well, Clodius Juba, that

* *lanista: trainer.*

turned out to be a very convenient training accident then, didn't it?'

Lucius had to admire his brother's audacity – but from the way Juba was now looking at him, Quin looked in serious danger of meeting with some kind of 'accident' himself. Then, unexpectedly, Juba's thick lips parted to reveal a mouthful of yellow, broken teeth. The lips spread further into a horrifying grin and great blasts of laughter exploded around the room. 'A soldier with a sense of humour!' he guffawed. 'I'm beginning to like you already!'

'We're after something Felix had in his possession.' Quin spoke sharply enough to cut through the din of the man's hysterics.

The laughter died. Juba's face returned to its former expression, full of placid malice. Lucius thought he looked like a cat comtemplating the torture of a small rodent.

'Some papers were entrusted to him by a friend,' said Quin. 'We need to reclaim those papers – on behalf of General Agricola.'

Juba picked at something in his teeth. 'Can you prove you're acting on his authority?' he asked.

Quin faltered. Lucius came to his rescue: 'Unfortunately, we were involved in an incident a few days ago,' he said, 'and the proconsul's official seal was lost…'

Juba looked the two of them up and down. 'Your story smells bad to me – a bit like the pong coming off your unwashed bodies. You don't exactly look like proconsular officials. You've got grass stains on your tunics, dents in your armour. I'll wager you're nothing but a pair of chancers who heard Felix had something valuable – something you want. Am I right?'

'No –' began Lucius.

'Well, I've taken possession of all of Felix's worldly goods. He owed me, see? Gambling debts. So the papers you want belong to me now.'

'Then you must hand them over,' insisted Quin. 'By order of the proconsul.'

This time Juba's laughter had a nasty, dangerous edge to it. 'You can drop the play-acting, son. No one ever gets the better of Clodius Galenus Juba. That's something you're going to have to learn.'

Lucius pulled the rolled-up lead tablet from his bag and handed it to Juba. 'This is a letter from Parmenion, the owner of the papers, giving us his permission to reclaim them.'

They both watched as Juba unfurled the tablet and frowned at it. Then he took a firm grip of the thin metal sheet in his powerful fists and ripped it in two. After that, he proceeded to rip it into quarters, and then into eighths. 'I don't read, sorry,' he chuckled as he flung the pieces away. 'If you want the papers so badly, pay me for them. Shall we say a hundred denarii?'*

Lucius stared bleakly at his brother. They had no more than a quarter of that between them.

---

* *denarii: small silver coins. One denarius was a day's wage for a labourer.*

'That's my price,' said Juba. 'If you can't pay, then clear off out of here. There are games starting tomorrow at the amphitheatre, and I need to get busy training my men.'

'Those papers are our property!' protested Lucius. 'They were only *entrusted* to Felix. He didn't own them, and so you don't either. So you have no right to ask for money for them.'

'So sue me!' said Juba, flashing them another broken-toothed grin. 'Oh, did I mention, the magistrate in this town also owes me money. That's why court cases in this city tend to get decided in my favour.'

Lucius felt his hopes starting to crumble. Juba reminded him of Silus, his old boss at the vivarium* in Rome: a small-time bully who used what little power he had to manipulate those around him. It was a waste of time even trying to appeal to the man's better nature, as he clearly didn't have one.

But Quin wasn't ready to give up. 'You say there are games starting tomorrow,' he said. 'Well, let me fight the best man you have.'

Lucius started in alarm as his brother took out their bag of remaining coins and threw it at Juba's feet. 'There are about twenty-five denarii in there. You can use that to bet on me winning.'

'Quin – no!' hissed Lucius.

'You'll get fantastic odds as I'm a complete unknown,' Quin continued. 'You can keep the stake

* *vivarium: a place where live animals are kept or raised.*

238

money and all the winnings. All we want is Parmenion's papers.'

Juba picked up the bag and weighed it in his hand. 'What kind of fighter are you?' he asked.

'A Retiarius,'* said Quin.

'And what if you lose?'

'Then you can have me as your slave. Either way, you'll end up a winner.'

Lucius couldn't believe what Quin was offering. He seemed determined to make them destitute, and himself a slave – and without more than a glimmer of hope that they would end up with the papers.

Juba's eyes sparkled as if the light of diamonds were reflecting in them. 'All right,' he said. 'I agree to the deal, but with one proviso. I want you both to fight.' He eyed the startled Lucius. 'From your physique I'm guessing that, like this one here, you are not a stranger to the art of single combat. If you both fight, that will double any potential profits for me.'

'Deal,' said Quin immediately.

Lucius felt as though he'd been punched. This was all so quick, so unexpected. His brother was risking everything, up to and including their lives, to get hold of those papers. And even if they won their fights, could they really trust this distinctly untrustworthy character to keep his side of the bargain and hand over the papers? It was a crazy gamble – and yet, when he thought about it, what choice did they have? There

* *Retiarius: a fighter with net and trident.*

was, in the end, only one way of getting what they wanted out of someone like Clodius Juba, and that was by appealing to his greed.

The amphitheatre of Londinium* was a large timber structure – a relic of the original, pre-Boudican city. Plans were already afoot to replace it with a more permanent stone structure as Londinium gradually transformed itself into a civilised Roman city – but for now the amphitheatre stood as a reminder of the city's wilder, frontier days, when it had survived precariously amid a landscape of hostile, barely subdued tribes. The sunken oval arena was surrounded by tiered seating supported by a tall latticework of thick timber struts founded on a raised bank of earth. It was a rickety, unsafe-looking building, Lucius thought, as he and Quin made the short walk towards it from the ludus. Built on sloping ground, it leaned at an eccentric angle. Its topmost tiers teetered, and its timbers creaked and strained as the denizens of Londinium mounted the external stairways to reach their seats. He heard raucous singing and chanting in bad Latin, and saw hordes of youths swilling flasks of mead. He'd seen passionate crowds in Carthage and Ephesus, but these were easily the noisiest and rowdiest of them all – and

* *the amphitheatre of Londinium: part of this building was excavated in 1987 and can be visited in the basement of the Guildhall Art Gallery.*

the gladiatorial entertainment hadn't even begun yet.

The two brothers were shown to a waiting area beneath the stands. It was one of two small antechambers located on either side of the passage that led into the arena. Another door with a small barred window led directly out onto the sandy oval. The room contained two wooden benches and two sets of armour and weapons. Here they would wait until called upon to fight. Quin, who was due on first, strapped a padded manica to his left arm – the only armour permitted to a Retiarius – then began practising his moves, flicking out his net and jabbing with his trident.

Meanwhile, Lucius positioned himself by the viewing window in the door and watched the show: a hairy, woad-covered Briton armed with a spear was attempting to kill – and avoid being killed by – a brown bear. Eventually, sickened by the death of the animal and the screeches of delight this provoked, Lucius turned away and went to lie down on one of the benches. 'Why are we doing this?' he asked. 'We're risking our lives in front of that mob, all for a document that might not even be enough to do the job. Glabrio's so strong now, I can't believe a piece of paper will be enough to bring him down.'

'I know why *I'm* doing it,' said Quin as he swirled his net towards an imaginary Secutor:* 'atonement.'

'Atonement?'

---

* *Secutor: a gladiator with gladius, shield and full-face helmet, the traditional opponent of a Retiarius.*

'Yeah. I wasn't there for Father in his hour of need. When he was accused of being the Spectre, I believed his accusers. I doubted him. I was disloyal. And for that, I can never forgive myself.'

'Father forgave you.'

Quin stopped and wiped a sheen of sweat from his forehead. 'I know, but it's not enough – not for me. I'm doing this for him, because I let him down. I'll shed my own blood if I have to. If I die, so be it – my only hope is that you'll survive to see this thing through.'

Lucius nodded. 'And if you don't die, what then?'

'What do you mean?'

'Say we win and we end up defeating Glabrio, what happens next? Will you enter the Senate as Father wanted?'

'Can you see me in that place?' chuckled Quin. Then he shook his head and frowned. 'I don't know. I can't imagine that far ahead. You know me, I'm a live-for-the-moment kind of guy.' He picked up his trident and began some slow overhand and underhand stabs. 'I do know one thing, though,' said Quin.

'What's that?'

'When all this is over, I'm going back to Caledonia and I'm going to find Floree and bring her back to Rome.'

'You're crazy,' laughed Lucius. 'She may not want to go with you. She may be married by then.'

Quin twirled his trident and smiled. 'I'm sure I can persuade her.'

His mention of Caledonia put Lucius in mind of another young woman. 'I may travel back there with you,' he said. 'See if I can persuade Isi to come back with me.'

'So what is it with you and Isi?' asked Quin. 'Just friends, or something more?'

'I don't know,' said Lucius. 'I have no idea what she thinks of me. One minute she's friendly, the next she's as cold and remote as that country she now calls home.'

'That's women for you,' chuckled Quin.

Lucius didn't smile. 'You talked about disloyalty to Father earlier,' he said. 'Well, I was disloyal to Isi. I sided with Eprius against her. Things haven't been the same since then between us. Maybe they never will be.'

'She likes you, bro – don't worry.'

'Then why did she stay in Caledonia?'

'Because she hates Rome and all it stands for. But she was torn – anyone could see that. She tried to persuade you to stay, didn't she?'

Lucius remembered the vision he'd had when he'd said goodbye to her. 'Maybe you and I should pack it all in and go and become Caledonian hill farmers,' he smiled.

Quin laughed loudly at this. 'Yeah, I can just see me in a colourful cloak and leggings with one of those long dangly moustaches – I guess it's more me than a senatorial toga, anyway.'

Juba loomed large in the doorway. He bared the yellow wreckage of his teeth in a wolfish grin. 'You're on,' he said to Quin.

'Good luck,' said Lucius as his brother picked up his weapons and headed for the door. A moment later, he watched him emerge into the arena alongside his opponent, a Secutor who stood more than a head taller than Quin. The Secutor's helmet was smooth polished silver with two menacing black eye holes. It had a crest at the top and a wide collar at the bottom to guard his neck. With his pale, almost white skin, and metal fishlike head, he looked like some monster of the deep, sunless sea. The crowd had worked themselves up into something approaching a frenzy on the appearance of the two gladiators – the first pair of the day. As they stood in the centre, the Secutor raised his arms in the air and nodded, turning slowly to acknowledge all sections of the oval amphitheatre. He was a local favourite, for sure, because the screams and cheers as he faced each part of the stand were almost deafening. When Quin tried to do likewise, he received an equally enthusiastic chorus of boos and hisses.

There was a similar reaction when they were introduced by the summa rudis.* The Secutor's name, Corbulo, was greeted with loud whoops and roars, as was the recounting of his record: eight wins and no defeats. Quin was introduced simply as Quintus. Juba, aiming to maximise his betting profits, had told

* *summa rudis: referee.*

the officials that he was a tiro of the Helvetii* – a tribe
not exactly noted for their gladiatorial prowess. When
the hordes of Corbulo fans heard this, they booed even
more loudly than before, and this time their boos were
mingled with laughter, for the Helvetii were the first
Gallic tribe to have been defeated by Julius Caesar,
and their name had become something of a byword
for military ineptitude. In the stands, the bookies were
slashing the odds on a Corbulo victory, just as Juba
had hoped.

A Secutor, so Quin often told Lucius, is almost
impossible to defeat when he's in balance, with his sword
and shield correctly placed. The trick, he explained, is
to get him off-balance with his body unshielded. And
when the fight began, this was exactly what Quin set
about doing. He approached the task with constant
quick thrusts and feints, always changing the angle
of attack to keep his opponent insecure and reactive.
Sometimes he stabbed overhand, using the long reach
of the trident to try to hit the opponent's helmet or
shoulder. Then he switched to underhand, aiming at
the sword hand, the torso and the top of the thigh.

But Corbulo was good, and he hit back with wild
swings of his sword that forced Quin to retreat out
of range. The Secutor then tried to turn defence into
attack, advancing on his opponent while still slashing
away with his sword. Yet Quin was simply too quick

* *tiro: a beginner, facing his first fight; Helvetii: a Gallic tribe or group of
tribes from the area that is now Switzerland.*

for him. He stood his ground and managed to dart in between Corbulo's swings with more thrusts towards vulnerable targets. In his practised hands, Quin was able to twirl the trident in mesmerising ways, usually in stabbing motions, but sometimes even swinging the butt end towards the Secutor's unshielded side. For the first time, the crowd fell quiet. It was a simmering sort of quiet, punctuated by catcalls and frustrated shouts of encouragement to the struggling Corbulo. Lucius sensed that many of the supporters were itching to jump into the arena themselves and attack this upstart Retiarius who dared to imagine himself better than their hero.

But the crowd could give Corbulo nothing more than their voices, and that didn't seem to be enough. Increasingly, the Secutor's restricted vision and lack of mobility began to tell against him. He started to make mistakes, allowing Quin to make a strike beneath his shield and land a trident prong in his thigh. Minutes later, Corbulo received a resounding whack to his side from the blunt end of the trident that nearly sent him sprawling. In his anger, he rushed at Quin, which was the moment Quin had been waiting for. He stabbed his trident downwards in front of the Secutor's rear foot, and the man collapsed. Quin now hurled his trident towards Corbulo's helmet, but the Secutor rolled aside with surprising swiftness and scrambled to his feet while Quin was still pulling his trident out of the sand.

The men circled each other once again, but the atmosphere between them had completely changed. Quin appeared relaxed and focused – full of coiled strength and lithe movement – while Corbulo looked breathless, unsure and dazed. The mood of the crowd had altered, too. The spectators were no longer uniformly passionate for Corbulo, but had splintered into groups. The majority were still loudly vocal for the Secutor, but many of the rest had become boisterous – mocking or cursing their former favourite. A few had even switched sides, and were now shouting for 'Quintus'. A chant began somewhere high in the stands. Lucius couldn't make out the words, but it was eliciting scattered laughter from some people in neighbouring seats.

Quin had yet to use his net. The problem with the net, as he used to tell Lucius, is that it's a one-shot weapon. If you cast it and miss, you've lost half your weaponry: you're just a half-naked man with a trident and no shield against an armoured opponent. So a lot of the skill of fighting as a Retiarius is knowing exactly when to throw the net. Lucius wasn't surprised that Quin was delaying his use of it. He needed to study his opponent first to know when the net might be most effective. Throughout the fight, Lucius was sure that Quin had been observing Corbulo, checking whether he led with his right or left foot, the positioning of his sword, and any quirks or 'tells' he exhibited. It was absolutely vital that the throw entangled the opponent thoroughly. A half-entangled Secutor could still be very dangerous.

Quin tried to draw Corbulo into an attack by lowering his trident, but the bigger man was understandably nervous. In the end, it was the mockery from sections of the crowd that stung him into action. He came at Quin suddenly, his sword slicing the air in front of him in violent crosses. Quin stepped lightly to one side and flicked his wrist. The net flared out towards Corbulo. Quin's flick imparted a spin that made the edges of the net fly outwards, fully opening it. The larger holes in the centre of the net entangled the Secutor's sword and upper body, while the finer, heavier mesh at the edges closed the net, trapping him. It was a perfect throw. Quin pulled hard at the string attached to the net, which was wound around his wrist, and the already unbalanced and confused Corbulo stumbled and fell to the ground. Almost immediately, a finger emerged from within the mesh of the net: Corbulo had surrendered.

There was a groan from the spectators. At the same time, the chanting from high in the stands grew louder, and now seemed to be spreading through other sections of the crowd. Lucius felt more than the usual elation at seeing his brother survive and triumph in a gladiatorial bout: this victory had extra significance because it meant they were halfway to achieving their goal. Mingled within his delight, however, was a sick feeling in the base of his stomach: now it was his turn to fight!

Once the Secutor had surrendered, he was no longer in any danger of death. He was far too popular with the locals, despite this defeat – and, besides, gladiators were far too rare and expensive a commodity in Britannia to be killed off so cheaply. The sponsor of the games duly offered up the shielded thumb of mercy, and Quin helped his defeated opponent out of his entanglement. Yet Lucius barely noticed the aftermath of the fight – he was too shocked by the words of the chant to take in much else. The chants were loud now – loud enough to be heard clearly in his little antechamber tucked in behind the arena wall – in fact, they rang out around half the amphitheatre: 'Hail, Phoenix of Pompeii – risen again!'

CHAPTER XIV

5 JUNE

ow? thought Lucius. *How could they know? Were there people here who had seen him fight in Rome or Pompeii and recognised him?* Quin had a style of his own, that was for sure, and his handsome features were well enough known in Latium and Campania* – Lucius had himself seen the graffiti sketches of his brother on the walls of Suburra – yet he was astonished that his fame could have spread as far as this distant outpost of the empire. And even if it had, surely no one really believed he could still be alive. Thousands had witnessed his funeral procession. Was the myth of his immortality so powerful that the people chanting out there really believed they'd just seen the Phoenix fight? Lucius had only begun to contemplate

* Latium: the area around Rome; Campania: the area that includes Pompeii.

the dangers that this new development could pose for them when a slave arrived and told him to armour up. He was on!

Trying to keep calm, he began putting on his Hoplomachus outfit. He donned his manica, greave and small shield, and put on his belt with his gladius and dagger sheathed in their scabbards. Then he picked up his spear and bronze helmet, mumbled a quick prayer to Fortuna* and stepped out onto the cool, grey Londinium sand.

For some reason, Clodius Juba was out there waiting for him, dressed to fight. What was going on?

Juba grinned, exposing his full array of evil dentistry. 'I'll bet you didn't expect to face me!' he chuckled. 'I may be a lanista now, but I'm still a fighter at heart.'

Lucius tried his best not to appear fazed. 'Betting against yourself, are you?' he asked.

'No, I would never do that,' Juba responded cheerfully. 'I bet on Quintus because he seemed confident and looked like he could handle himself. It proved a wise investment, and I've made a pretty packet out of him today. But I didn't appreciate his insinuation that I killed Favonius Felix to become lanista. So I thought I'd punish him by depriving him of his little brother!'

Lucius's blood chilled a few degrees. 'How did you know we were brothers?'

* _Fortuna: goddess of good and bad luck._

Again, Juba's face was split by that friendly, horrifying grin. It reminded Lucius of the dreadful crescent of fire he'd seen descending the slope of Vesuvius moments before Pompeii was engulfed. 'There's little that gets past Clodius Juba,' said the lanista. 'I was listening in on your conversation in the waiting room earlier…'

Lucius prayed he hadn't heard any references to their plans for Glabrio – Juba had the distinct look of a blackmailer about him. Still, none of that would matter if Juba succeeded in his aim of killing him.

The sand had been raked over, and the summa rudis summoned the combatants to the centre of the arena. Juba was big and brutish, with the cunning air of a streetfighter about him. Lucius was sure he'd fight the way he lived his life: dishonourably – doing whatever it took to win.

Chants for Quin continued to reverberate around the ground.

'Your brother,' grunted Juba. 'Is he really the Phoenix?'

'No,' said Lucius immediately. 'The Phoenix is dead. They've made a mistake.'

Juba smiled slyly, but said nothing. When they reached the middle of the arena, the summa rudis presented them to the crowd. Juba was introduced as a Gallus or Gaul, an ancient species of gladiator, extinct in Italia, but still seen from time to time in the provinces. He was armed in Gallic fashion, with a gladius and a scutum – a large, rectangular shield that curved round protectively, like a legionary's shield. He wore a bright yellow loincloth, a fancy metal greave on his lower left leg and a leather manica on his meaty forearm and wrist. On his head he wore an open-faced, bell-shaped, crested helmet called a galea.

'Twenty fights and no losses!' boomed the summa rudis, summarising Juba's career to date. Lucius felt his insides turn to slimy mush. This man would destroy him! Juba raised his arms and acknowledged the cheers, which were a good deal less enthusiastic than they'd been for Corbulo. But this didn't encourage Lucius – the opposite, in fact. Gladiators were usually unpopular for one of two reasons: either they weren't local, or they fought dirty. Juba was, of course, a local…

The summa rudis introduced Lucius as an unbeaten veteran of ten fights. The lanista had, once again, lied to the administrators about the combatant's record to suit himself – in this case because he didn't want anyone to think he was awarding himself an easy contest. Yet, to judge from the laughter that greeted this announcement, Juba may have miscalculated – it was clear that few believed that someone as young as Lucius could possibly boast such a record.

The summa rudis called for the fight to begin. Lucius put on his helmet and experienced the familiar, sickening sensation of the world closing in around him. His breath, already sharp and shaky, echoed loud in his ears, and with his vision restricted to the view from two small eye holes, he was forced to move his head from side to side, to make up for the loss of lateral vision. The sight of Juba advancing upon him caused a deep shiver, and brought fresh droplets of sweat to his face. He clutched his spear tight and raised his shield.

Juba raised his sword to strike, and Lucius feinted to his left. The Gallus swivelled to cut off his escape and swung down his sword arm. But Lucius swayed to the right, and the blade hissed through empty air.

The big man growled: 'You can duck and weave all you like, but you can't escape me forever.'

Lucius jabbed his spear towards Juba's shoulder, testing out the lanista's reflexes. Juba parried easily with his shield, and then moved once more into the attack, swinging his sword in violent slashes as he advanced. Lucius retreated, but couldn't draw back his spear in time. The gladius blade passed clean through the shaft, severing the iron tip and turning the spear into a short, useless wooden staff. The crowd cheered this dramatic development, and Juba laughed. Scared and frustrated, Lucius flung the spear away and drew his gladius. In the back of his mind, he wondered at how easily Juba had destroyed the weapon. Had he tampered with it beforehand, weakening it in some way?

Lucius got his sword into position just in time to parry a series of hard blows from Juba. The Gallus came at him from above and below, and from side to side. Lucius reacted instinctively, no longer thinking, just allowing his reflexes to move his limbs into position as he blocked Juba's assault with his sword and small shield. Juba was driving him steadily backwards towards the arena wall, where a guard was standing over a brazier with a red-hot branding iron. From the excited grin on the lanista's face, Lucius could see that he planned to send him careering backwards, right into the brazier. The scorching wounds he'd receive would be enough to end the contest and maybe his life. Soon, Lucius could feel the blistering heat of the coals against the skin of his back. Sensing victory, Juba increased the speed and intensity of his assault, leaving Lucius with no choice but to yield yet more ground. The force of the blows was jarring his arms painfully. He was sure his shoulder would go numb any second and he might even lose his sword.

Lucius tried desperately to push back against Juba's sword, then felt a ridge of hard, screamingly hot metal against his lower back. He cried out in pain as Juba tried to barge him into the brazier with his shield. Lucius felt himself toppling backwards. He made a desperate grab for the edge of Juba's shield, pulling with all his might, determined to take the big man with him. Juba tried to jerk himself free, and this gave Lucius the leverage he needed to twist himself out of danger. He threw himself to the side and rolled across the sand before scrambling to his feet. A line of agony ran across his lower back.

They stared at each other across a span of four paces. 'I can end the pain for you now, soldier boy,' snarled Juba. 'Or do you want me to take my time killing you?'

Lucius said nothing. He squeezed his eyes shut and blinked away the tears. It was a strip of pure bright torture across his back.

'I never had any intention of giving you or your brother those papers,' Juba smirked. 'If they're so valuable, I'll sell them myself – once I've killed you, that is. And if your brother makes trouble, I'll kill him, too.'

When he heard this, Lucius went very still. He felt his blood turn cold. At that moment, his dislike of the man swelled into hatred. His anger ballooned into rage. He felt his jaw clench and his muscles flex and quiver. Fresh energy, borne on a tide of loathing, poured into his limbs. As Juba's sword swept towards him once again, he met it with a low parry. A strangled yowl rose from his throat as he forced it upwards, twisting Juba's wrist back in the process. Juba's eyes widened in surprise as he was forced to take a backward step. Then Lucius let forth an animal roar and flew at him. In a frenzy of violence, he hacked and slashed at the lanista, forcing him to retreat. Within the cauldron of his hatred, a cooler part of Lucius's mind remained detached, quietly observing. He imagined his body as a tool of destruction – a weapon unleashing shock and fury on his opponent. He could taste the sour froth of saliva in his mouth, feel the slick coating of sweat on his skin, the line of pain across his back and the fierce ache in his arms and legs and shoulders as he drove them on – but he experienced these things almost as though they were part of someone else.

Juba's defences began to crumble beneath the onslaught. Lucius's sword bit into the flesh of the lanista's sword arm, making him cry out. Juba, eyes now maddened with pain, hit back, shoving his shield hard into Lucius's face. Lucius heard a crack in his nose and tasted blood. He staggered backwards, fresh pain momentarily clouding all thought. A sixth sense alerted him to Juba's follow-up sword strike. He blocked it inches before it sliced into his thigh. Then he felt another crack – though this time no pain. The sword felt different in his hand – unbalanced. As he raised it to block another attack from Juba, he saw a jagged split running all the way through the blade. When Juba struck, there was a ghastly screech of tearing metal, and Lucius's sword sheared through the middle. More than half the blade fell to the ground, leaving Lucius with nothing more than a blunt and useless stump, shorter than a dagger.

There was a groan from the crowd – but not one of surprise. Lucius guessed that this sort of misfortune had befallen Juba's opponents before. Frustrated beyond endurance, he hurled the remnant of the weapon at his adversary. It bounced harmlessly off his shield. Then Lucius drew his pugio, the last of his three weapons, already suspecting with sinking heart that Juba had tampered with this as well. But Juba hadn't needed to – in a contest between sword and dagger there can only ever be one winner. With an arrogant sweep of his gladius, Juba knocked the pugio out of Lucius's hand. And there the young gladiator stood, defenceless against his much larger adversary.

Juba's face widened into a savage grin. Blood welled from his shoulder, but he seemed to have forgotten the wound in his excitement at the closeness of victory. As they stared at each other, the sun unexpectedly broke through from its covering of clouds, bathing the arena in cool, silvery light. Juba advanced, raising his sword to deliver the killing stroke. Lucius backed up, keeping his eyes fastened on those of his opponent, waiting for the flicker in their depths that would indicate he was about to strike. All Lucius had left now was his reflexes. But he couldn't fool himself: he knew the end was coming, and soon. His strength was failing, and the pain in his nose and back was now returning to eclipse everything else – including the hate-fuelled energy that had driven him to this point. Juba would kill him, for sure – he wouldn't wait for the verdict of the crowd or the sponsor. Lucius tried to maintain his distance from Juba, moving backwards on a curving line, but it was getting increasingly difficult, as Juba's longer stride meant that he was always closing the gap. Now the lanista was within sword-striking distance, and

Lucius had run out of room to retreat, with the arena wall now at his back. He was exhausted, his brain no longer able to feed his body instructions. Juba spread his lips in an ecstatic smile and drew back the elbow of his sword arm to drive the blade into Lucius's chest.

As he did so, something very bright flashed in his eyes. Juba blinked and hesitated. In that second, Lucius's senses returned, and he struck. His shield smashed into Juba's jaw. The big man staggered backwards, the light still blindingly bright in his eyes. Lucius kicked at his knee and Juba keeled over, dropping his sword as he fell. Moving very quickly now, Lucius scooped up the sword from the sand and pointed its tip at Juba's throat. Juba emitted a bellow of rage and tried to wriggle out from beneath the blade, but Lucius pressed the tip harder into his throat, breaking the skin. Juba's jaw dropped open and he whined with fear.

The crowd had become hysterical. They were yelling for Juba's blood, so Lucius had to raise his voice to make himself heard. 'Promise me you'll give us the papers,' he yelled at Juba, 'or I'll kill you now!'

'I promise!' cried Juba.

But, of course, Lucius didn't believe him. 'If you don't, I'll tell everyone that you sabotaged my weapons.'

'I'll give you the damn papers!' the lanista screamed.

The crowd's demands for death were clearly agitating the sponsor. Shakily, he offered the shielded thumb – a decision condemned by a hail of boos and whistles that resounded for some minutes around the amphitheatre. Lucius wondered whether the sponsor, like the city magistrates, was under Juba's influence.

He released Juba, who pushed aside his proffered helping hand and climbed sullenly to his feet. As Lucius raised his hand to acknowledge the cheers of his new-won fans, he cast his eye back towards the seats behind him to try and work out what could have caused the fortuitous blaze of light that had dazzled his opponent. But he could see nothing there apart from row upon row of smiling, cheering spectators. It was oddly reminiscent of what had happened to Baltair during the fight with Quin when Isi had used her mirror to…

That was when the idea struck him. But it was impossible, surely. She was some four hundred miles* away to the north, in Caledonia… He studied the position of the sun in the sky, and saw that it was gleaming through a gap in the clouds just above the stand on the far side of the amphitheatre – directly *behind* where Juba had been standing. A mirror was the only possible explanation. Scanning the crowds behind him once again, he tried to find Isi somewhere among them, but there was no sign of her.

---

* *four hundred (Roman) miles: 590 kilometres.*

Two hours later, Quin and Lucius entered Juba's office in the ludus. The bleeding from Lucius's nose had finally stopped, and the pain had subsided to a dull throb, but it now had a distinctly squashed appearance and he feared it would never return to its former shape. As for his back, the medicus had treated it with honey and placed a bandage over the blistering skin, yet it remained very sore.

They found a very different Juba behind the desk. Gone was the self-satisfied smirk. The lanista simply sat there looking surly and resentful, rubbing his freshly bandaged shoulder. 'What do you want?' he spat.

'We've fulfilled our side of the deal,' said Quin. 'Now hand us the papers.'

Juba didn't budge from his seat. 'I want money first.'

'You've had our money,' said Quin, 'every last sestertius.* And you've had all the winnings you made on my fight – just as we agreed.'

'You cheated,' snarled Juba. 'You put someone in the stands with a mirror to blind me.'

Quin hurled himself at the lanista then, leaping onto the desk and pushing him backwards so that his chair and the back of his head hit the wall behind. By the time the stunned Juba knew what was happening, he had the tip of a pugio pointing at his throat.

'You're a fine one to talk about cheating, you dog,'

---

* sestertius: a large brass coin worth a quarter of a denarius.

Quin hissed in his ear. 'We've checked out those weapons you gave my brother and they were clearly tampered with. We can show the evidence to the officials of the games if you like, or you can hand over the papers right now!'

'Guards!' Juba groaned feebly.

Quin jabbed at the already cut skin of the lanista's throat. 'You'll be dead before anyone arrives,' he warned. 'Now give us what's ours.'

With the prompt of Quin's knife in his side, Juba jerked to his feet and made for an arched opening shrouded by a grubby curtain at the back of his office. Quin followed close behind, keeping the knife tip pressed to his back so Juba could feel it through his tunic. Behind the curtained portal lay a storeroom full of odds and ends that Juba had evidently collected from his dead or non-paying debtors. Among them was a small, leather-covered wooden chest, which he handed to Quin. 'The papers are in there,' he said.

Quin tried to open it, but found it was locked. 'Is there a key?' he asked.

Scowling, Juba returned to his office and removed a key from a bowl on his desk. The key was attached to a ring.

'I found this on Felix's finger when he died,' he said.

Quin placed the chest on the desk, inserted the key into the lock and turned it. The lid opened. There were two scrolls inside.

Lucius's hands were shaking as he unfurled

the larger one. He recognised Parmenion's script immediately:

Idibus Septembribus DCCCXXXIV AUC*

I, Diomedes, physician, do hereby swear by Aesculapius** that the following report is true. I was witness to the death of Emperor Titus Flavius Caesar Vespasianus Augustus, which occurred on this day at duodecima hora.*** My observations of the emperor during his final hours and my subsequent examination of his body post mortem are described in detail below. They lead me to the inescapable conclusion that the cause of the emperor's death was poisoning. Since the poison in question was Atropa belladonna, *a plant not used in any known recipe and not native to the locality in which the emperor was residing at the time of his death, accidental ingestion of the poison was not possible. I must therefore conclude that the poisoning was deliberately carried out by a person or persons unknown.*

The report went on for several more paragraphs, describing in detail the physician's observations and post-mortem examination. But Lucius didn't need to read any further. The opening paragraph told him all he needed to know. His voice shook with emotion as he told Quin: 'This is it. This is what we need.'

---

* *Idibus . . . AUC: on the Ides of Sptember in the 834th year since the founding of the city (= 13 September, AD 81).*

** *Aesculapius: god of medicine.*

*** *duodecima hora: the 12th hour of the day – the last hour of daylight.*

'Then you can hand it straight over to me,' said a sharp, well-spoken voice from the other side of the room.

All three whirled round, and Lucius let out an involuntary groan when he saw who it was.

'Lurco,' sighed Quin.

The military tribune was standing by the door, accompanied by half a dozen armed legionaries. He appeared in surprisingly good health, considering the state they'd left him in at Aquae Sulis. His right hand was now a hook of gleaming steel, but apart from that, he was his usual immaculate self, dressed in polished armour that had never seen a battlefield, and an impressive scarlet cloak.

Addressing the surprised Juba, Lurco said: 'Lanista, I am Appius Mallius Lurco, military tribune based at Pinnata Castra in Caledonia. I don't know what these men have told you, but I can assure you that they are imposters, posing as legionaries. They are, in fact, dangerous renegades wanted for treason back in Rome.' Then he turned on Lucius and Quin: 'Quintus Valerius Felix, Lucius Valerius Aquila, I arrest you both on the orders of the consul Marcus Acilius Glabrio. And you can also hand over that box of treasonous papers.'

Lurco and his soldiers moved further into the room. The legionaries surrounded Lucius and Quin, cutting off all escape routes. Quin had put the scroll back in the leather box, which he was now clutching protectively to his chest.

A smirk had, by now, reappeared on Juba's face. 'I had a feeling there was something not quite right about these two, Tribune,' he said. 'I've got an instinct about that sort of thing, you know. But when I refused to give them those papers, that one went and put a knife to my throat. Forced me to hand them over.' With a glint of yellow teeth, he added: 'I held out for as long as I could. If it hadn't been for me, they'd be long gone by now. Not that I'm thinking about a reward or anything. Just doing my duty as a Roman citizen, you understand…'

'You'll be compensated for your trouble, lanista, don't worry,' said Lurco, keeping his eyes fixed on Quin and the chest he was holding.

'Thank you, sir,' said Juba, bowing obsequiously.

From somewhere down the corridor, near the entrance to the ludus, came a clamour of excited shouts and cries.

'Hand it over!' Lurco snapped at Quin.

Quin didn't move.

Lurco nodded to a couple of the soldiers. One grabbed Quin and placed the tip of his sword blade to his neck, while the other one siezed the chest, forcing it from his fingers.

Lucius felt crushed. All the hopes that had carried them two thousand miles* since leaving Rome lay in that chest. He couldn't believe that they'd come so far,

---

* *two thousand (Roman) miles = 2,960 kilometres.*

and got so close, only to see it snatched away from them at the last moment.

'Now, kill them!' ordered Lurco.

The soldier with his sword to Quin's throat glanced back at Lurco to make sure he hadn't misheard.

The shouting in the corridor had grown louder, accompanied by the thunder of hundreds of running footsteps. From a wild and scattered noise, the voices had cohered into a rhythmic chant. Lucius immediately recognised the words.

Hail, Phoenix of Pompeii – risen again!

A couple of the soldiers glanced out into the corridor and turned pale with shock.

'Guards!' cried the now panic-stricken Juba. 'Guards! Who let this mob in?'

'Kill them!!' screamed Lurco. 'Now!!!'

Even now the soldier hesitated.

'What are you waiting for?' cried Lurco. 'Do you want me to do it myself?' He pushed the soldier aside and began grappling with Quin.

A short, hooded figure appeared at the door at the head of a dense pack of people – it was impossible to say how many.

Quin took advantage of the distraction to break free of Lurco's grip.

'Don't let them in!' screamed Juba.

But before the soldiers could draw their swords, the mob burst into the room. There were over a dozen of them, with many more pushing in from behind.

The hooded figure was leading the chant, banging a staff on the ground to generate a rhythm: *Ave Phoenix Pompeiorum – resurrectus! Hail, Phoenix of Pompeii – risen again!*

A few of the new arrivals recognised Quin and immediately made for him, breaking through the cordon of soldiers as if they weren't there. The soldiers were spun around dizzily, and Lurco was pushed unceremoniously aside. A couple of big men hoisted Quin onto their shoulders and began to carry him back out through the doorway. Lucius seized back the chest from the limp hands of a shocked legionary and followed Quin and the rest of the parade out of the door.

'Stop them!' shrieked Lurco, but he was barely heard by his dazed and trampled troops.

The procession filed out of the ludus and into a sunny Londinium afternoon. More people joined them there, and the crowd grew so big that they filled the street from side to side. Cloaked by such a large throng, Lucius felt anonymous and safe as he held the precious little wooden chest tightly beneath his arm. Everyone around him was laughing with excitement, as if they'd witnessed a genuine and joyful miracle, and Lucius couldn't help joining in. It did seem to him like a miracle – that Quin's fame could spread so far, and that a spontaneous celebration of his return could end up saving the day for them. He saw Quin nearby, borne aloft by a human river, covered in flower petals that were being tossed at him from all directions. He was laughing as much as everyone else, and there were tears in his eyes – he was clearly moved by all the love they were heaping on him.

Lucius was determined to discover the identity of the mysterious leader of the demonstration, so he pushed his way through to the front of the crowd. As he got closer, he saw that the hooded figure was carrying a staff in his right hand and a bronze mirror in his left. When Lucius saw the mirror, his heart started beating extremely fast. He would have recognised that mirror anywhere.

He rushed up to the figure and pulled back the hood.

A familiar olive-brown face looked up at him, her expression of surprise quickly turning to joy.

'Isi!' he cried, hugging her. 'I knew it was you! It had to be you!' He was so effusive, he stopped her in her tracks, causing those immediately behind to stumble into her.

'Let me go!' she cried breathlessly. 'We can't stop now.'

With a happy sigh, Lucius released her and they continued to march at the head of the procession, Isi banging her staff in time with the chanting.

'You shone your mirror in Juba's eyes, didn't you?' he said.

Isi smiled. 'I did.'

'You saved my life with that thing, just like you

saved Quin's life before… But how did you manage to organise a demonstration like this?'

'I didn't,' she said. 'It was happening anyway, outside the amphitheatre. But then I saw those soldiers heading into the ludus, and I guessed they were coming for you, so I shouted to all the Quin fans that their hero was in the building, and luckily they all followed me. It was the only way I could think of to rescue you.'

As evening fell in Londinium, the parade turned into a street party. Many of them urged Quin, Lucius and Isi to join them, but the trio knew they couldn't remain in Londinium. By now, Lurco was bound to have given their descriptions to the local urban cohorts* and ordered the arrest of these 'dangerous renegades'. Their safest course of action, they decided, was to board the next ship out of there. As they made their way through the back streets towards the port of Londinium, Isi related her tale to the other two.

'It wasn't long', she said, 'before I regretted my decision to stay at the Caledonian settlement. The day after you left, I was spotted by one of the men there while I was washing myself. Once they knew I was a girl, they were no longer interested in me as a warrior or as a trainer of warriors. They only thought of me as a potential wife for one of their clansmen. So as soon as

* *urban cohorts: security forces.*

I could, I made my escape and found my way back to the fort. The sentries at the gate told me that you two had departed, taking the southern road. I assumed you were going back to Rome, so I headed for Londinium, hoping I might catch up with you before you shipped out of here. I might have known I'd find you boys fighting for your lives in an arena!'

'Well, your timing was perfect,' said Quin.

'Thank you.'

Quin blushed a little as he asked his next question: 'Did you, um, have a chance to chat with Floree?'

'We talked a bit,' said Isi with an enigmatic smile.

'And did she happen to mention me?'

'She asked me to tell her all about you.'

'And what did you say?'

'I told her you were arrogant and to be avoided at all costs.'

Quin stared at her, horrified.

'I'm joking,' smirked Isi. 'I told her you were a famous gladiator and charioteer, and very brave – if a little hot-headed at times. She seemed to like what she heard... It was Floree who helped me escape, by the way. She wanted to come with me, but I told her it was a bad idea.'

'You did *what*?' Quin thundered.

'Think about it,' said Isi. 'You'd only put her in danger if she joined us now. Do you really want that?'

Quin clenched his jaw. 'I'll go back there one day,' he said determinedly. 'I'll bring her to Rome.'

By now, they had arrived at the waterfront. They sat down on the stone quayside and looked out across the wide river. A long wooden bridge disappeared into a misty gloom to the south. It was nearing the end of the day, but the docks were still busy: a number of large merchant ships had arrived on the tide and were now lying at anchor in the middle of the river while their cargoes were conveyed to shore in lighter vessels. On the wharf, dockworkers unloaded crates and amphorae of luxury foods, wine, fine pottery, jewellery and glassware – goods as yet unavailable in this uncivilised land.

The river was calm, the last rays of the sun shining flecks of pale gold on its green ripples. The pink tiles and white walls of the newly built warehouses glowed softly in the same dying light. Lucius mouthed a prayer of thanks to Apollo, god of the sun, for without his timely appearance that afternoon, Isi's mirror trick could not have saved him.

'I'm glad you're here now,' he said to Isi. 'It wasn't the same without you.'

'Well, I thought you boys could probably do with a little help,' she said.

'So you weren't tempted to marry a handsome young Caledonian, then?' he asked.

'Are you kidding?' laughed Isi. 'Marriage! Yuck!'

'Besides,' she added, leaning over and kissing him on the cheek, 'if I got married, I'd miss out on all these fantastic adventures with you.'

END OF BOOK 5

AUTHOR'S NOTE

In this book, I have interwoven my story with a real-life historical event: the Roman invasion of Caledonia – or Scotland, as it is known today. In the course of the story, two real historical characters make an appearance: Gnaeus Julius Agricola, governor of Britannia and commander of the Roman forces during the invasion, and Calgacus, the Caledonian leader of an alliance of tribes who fought against the Romans. A character in this book called Cornix is sceptical of the Romans' ability to conquer Caledonia. Yet just two years later, in AD 84, Agricola would decisively defeat Calgacus's forces at the battle of Mons Graupius. However, Cornix would be proved right in the long term: in AD 122, forty years after the events of this book, the emperor Hadrian (reigned 117–138) decided to withdraw Roman forces more than 160 kilometres south of Pinnata Castra (now Inchtuthil, Perthshire), building a wall there to mark the northern limit of Roman Britain. Over the next hundred years, Emperors Antoninus Pius (138–161) and Septimius Severus (193–211) tried to re-establish a presence to the north of Hadrian's Wall, but both attempts ended in failure. For the Romans, Caledonia would prove a conquest too far.

I have endeavoured in this book to depict Britannia as it was in AD 82, just thirty-nine years after invasion and very near the beginning of the 367-year occupation. I imagine the province would have been far from fully Romanised by that stage, and the occupying forces would probably have felt insecure and a long way from home. The famous sites of Roman Britain, such as the fort of Vindolanda near Hadrian's Wall and the Great Bath at Aquae Sulis (Bath), have yet to be built, and Londinium's amphitheatre is still a rickety timber construction. Occasionally, I have altered things slightly for the sake of my story. The sacred spring at Aquae Sulis was not enclosed within a barrel-vaulted building until the second century AD, and would have been simply an open pool at the time of Lucius and Quin's visit. However, that particular scene would not have worked so well in an outdoor setting.

FOLLOW LUCIUS'S FURTHER ADVENTURES IN:

GLADIATOR SCHOOL 6
BLOOD JUSTICE

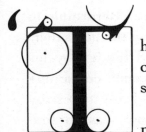 here's someone following us, I'm sure of it,' said Lucius, glancing over his shoulder.

'Well then don't look at him,' muttered Quin. 'Keep facing forwards.' His hand moved to the hilt of his sword, a habitual reflex whenever danger threatened.

'It can't be far now, can it?' asked Isi.

The boys didn't reply, their minds preoccupied with the mysterious shadow to their rear. Lucius was absolutely sure that someone was there. Yet when he risked another peek behind him, he could see no one suspicious among the bustling crowds of pedestrians.

They were back in Rome. Their ship had docked that morning, and they were now walking along the

Alta Semita, a road taking them northeast towards the Quirinal Hill. It was a hot day, and the smells of the city were always at their worst on days like this: smells of sewage, sweat and manure wafted in from Suburra to the south.

It was a nerve-racking experience being back in Rome. This was where Consul Glabrio's power was at its strongest. Glabrio was their mortal enemy. He had killed the boys' father, Aquila, and was now determined to kill them. Here, above all, he had the means to do so. He wielded great influence over the new emperor, Domitian, and he controlled the emperor's elite troops, the Praetorian Guard. He dominated the Senate and had spies and informers everywhere. Returning to Rome was, in many ways, like entering the lion's den.

Tucked beneath Lucius's arm and hidden by his cloak was the small leather-covered casket containing the evidence that he hoped they could use to destroy Glabrio. All they needed to do now was to find someone with sufficient stature, integrity and courage to present the evidence against Glabrio in court. The one man in Rome who possessed all of these qualities, and who would be prepared to stand up to Glabrio, was Senator Aulus Pomponius Licinius. It was to Licinius's residence on the Quirinal Hill that they were now heading.

They passed through the Porta Sanqualis in the Servian Wall, the six-hundred-year-old defensive barrier that surrounded the inner part of the city, and began the steep climb up the hill. They passed temples and ancient, mossy tombs, some of them dating back to the early Sabine settlers on the hill, before the founding of Rome. After cool, damp Britannia, the heat of the Roman summer was hard to tolerate, and very soon their under-tunics were damp with sweat. Before their arrival in Rome, Lucius and Quin had swapped their legionary uniforms for togas, and Isi had replaced hers with a ladylike stola. That way they were less likely to stand out, and the formal clothing gave them a status that would hopefully allow them access to a man such as Licinius.

Senator Licinius lived on the fashionable north side of the Quirinal, where many of Rome's wealthy patrician class had their homes. The house was an imposing, red-brick structure built into the side of the hill. Lucius was reassured by the size and bulk of the property. Here, he was certain, lived a man who would be able to help them. They therefore felt reasonably confident as they approached the doorway of the house.

Then Isi stopped.

'Cypress branches,' she said.

'What?' said Quin.

She pointed. A dark fear entered Lucius's heart as he took in the sight of the cypress boughs placed above the fine arched entrance.

They were the sign of a house in mourning.

They knocked on the door, and the porter, wearing

dark colours and a solemn expression, opened it.

'Is the master at home?' Quin asked.

'The master', the porter informed them, 'is dead.'

As he heard these words, Lucius felt a heavy weight dragging him down into the earth.

Of course he was dead! What did they expect? Everyone who opposed Glabrio ended up dead!

Aulus Pomponius Licinius, they learned from the porter, had met with an appalling accident only a few days earlier. While out boar-hunting in the Sabine Hills to the northeast of the city, one of his companions had accidentally speared him.

Shock and depression filled all three of them as they dragged themselves away from Licinius's house. Whether it really was an accident, or murder made to seem like one, the end result was the same: Licinius, the only man capable of helping them, was no more. Lucius felt, more than ever before, a sense of powerlessness. Perhaps they were in over their heads. Glabrio had all the forces of the state to draw upon, while he, Quin and Isi had virtually nothing – just two flimsy parchment scrolls. It seemed as though they had reached a dead end. For the first time, Lucius couldn't think what to do next.

Under a cloud of gloom, they descended the north side of the hill down a winding, tree-lined path, and entered the Gardens of Sallust. This manicured landscape of walkways, sculptures, lawns and flowerbeds, which lay between the Quirinal and

Pincian Hills, failed to lift their spirits. They sat on a bench, wiped their sweat-drenched faces and tried to decide on their next move. Quin was all for going to the praetor and presenting the evidence to him. The praetor was the city's senior magistrate. He would have the power to call a trial.

'But he's almost certainly under the thumb of Glabrio, like every other official in Rome,' pointed out Lucius. 'If we go to the praetor's office, you can bet your life they'll treat us as the guilty ones. They'll arrest us and put us on trial for treason.'

'But a trial is exactly what we want!' insisted Quin. 'We can use the opportunity to show the documents in public.'

'They'd never allow it,' said Lucius. 'The documents will be destroyed and we'll be declared guilty and executed before any of the real story is allowed to leak out.'

'Are you saying there isn't a single person in this city whom we can trust?'

'There might be,' said Lucius, 'but we have no way of knowing who it is. I think we should lie low for a while – hide out somewhere until we can find someone who can help us.'

'And every day we delay, Glabrio gets stronger…' scowled Quin, thumping his fist against the stone seat of the bench.

Lucius knew how much his brother hated inaction – but what other choice did they have?

'And don't forget,' Quin added, 'he's going to marry Mother soon, and then our family's property will officially pass into his hands. Even if we manage to kill or disgrace him, we'll have a devil of a job trying to wrest what's ours from his heirs and descendants.'

Lucius had to admit that this was a good point. Time was definitely not on their side.

'We could try and scare him,' suggested Isi.

'How?' asked Lucius.

'By going out into the streets at night and painting pictures of Glabrio stabbing Titus in the back with the words "emperor killer" underneath…'

'Now there's an idea!' said Quin, a smile at last dawning on his face.

Isi wasn't finished: 'And we could try taking advantage of your fame, Quin. You saw what happened in Londinium, so far from the scene of your great victories. Imagine what would happen if people around here found out you were still alive! You know how much they love you in this city – particularly the poor. What if we start rumours in the slums of Suburra that the Phoenix of Pompeii is alive and well and is coming to exact revenge on Glabrio? Just imagine the shiver of terror that would give him when he hears about it. He might control the senators and the Praetorians – but, if we play this one right, we could control the mob.'

Quin's eyes lit up at the sound of this. 'By the gods, you're right, Isi! That's exactly what we should do!

We should appeal directly to the people of Rome. When we show them the proof of Glabrio's guilt, it could lead to a full-scale riot. Glabrio won't know what hit him.'

'Hold on,' said Lucius. 'Wouldn't all that draw attention to ourselves? He doesn't know we're here yet, and we could use that to our advantage…'

'Shhh!' hissed Quin suddenly.

'What is it?' asked Lucius, looking around.

Quin drew his sword and began moving in a crouched posture towards a statue on the other side of the path. 'Thought I saw someone moving behind there,' he whispered. 'Maybe it's the same person who was shadowing us earlier.'

The white marble statue was known as 'The Dying Gaul'.* It showed the slumped figure of a man with a sword wound in his chest. The man's wild hair and moustache, and the torc around his neck, reminded Lucius of the natives he'd encountered in Britannia. For a second he thought he saw a dark, blurred movement just behind the Gaul's right shoulder. Quin crept closer, so that he was close to the Gaul's knee. Then he suddenly pounced, like a cat, diving right over the statue and smothering whoever was lurking behind it. There came a squeal of fright, and Quin rose to his feet, dragging with him a thin, lanky figure. He had grasped the young man by the neck of his toga, while at the same time pointing the tip of his sword

---

* 'The Dying Gaul': a real statue found in the Gardens of Sallust.

towards his cheek.

'Why are you spying on us?' Quin growled. 'One of Glabrio's men, are you? Planning to sneak off and tell your master where we are?'

'N-n-n,' was all the terrified young man could stutter.

'Speak if you value your life!' roared Quin.

'P-p-please,' said the man. 'D-d-don't kill me. I'm a f-f-friend.'

Quin let the sword drop to his side. The young man was unarmed and clearly no threat to them. Yet Quin continued to hold him by the scruff, in case he tried to make a run for it.

'Who are you?' Lucius asked.

The young man cleared his throat and tried to draw himself up to his full not-very-impressive height. He was a boy of perhaps Lucius's age, but a good deal shorter and slighter of build. 'I am Gaius Horatius Canio,' he said, 'son of the late Galerius Horatius Canio.'

Senator Canio, as they all knew, was the only witness, besides Aquila, to the murder of Titus.

Lucius stared hard at him, and began to discern faint similarities between the boy standing before them and the senator whom he'd met for the last time in Ephesus three months earlier. The boy had the same round face and earnest expression as his father.

'I apologise for following you,' said the boy. 'But I had to be certain that you were the people I've been searching for. You see, I want the same as you: revenge. And if we act together, I think we can do it. We can destroy Marcus Acilius Glabrio.'

TO BE CONTINUED...

WARRIORS AND

Caledonian warrior
Weapons: long sword and spear
Shield: long, oval
Helmet: metal and leather
Armour: none
Opponents: the Romans and,
    sometimes, other British
    tribes

Postulatus, 'the Favourite'
Weapons: mace or flail, and sword
Shield: none
Helmet: full-face with grille-covered
    eye holes
Armour: manica (arm guard),
    greaves (shin guards)
Opponents: Noxii (criminals), in
    special display fights before
    the emperor

GLADIATORS

Roman legionary
Weapons: spear (pilum), short
  sword (gladius), dagger (pugio)
Shield: large, rectangular, curved
Helmet: domed, with neck and
  cheek protectors
Armour: cuirass (breastplate) of
  metal hoops over leather
Opponents: anyone who threatens
  the borders of the Roman empire

Gregarius, 'the Common Gladiator'
Weapon: probably spear or sword
Shield: none
Helmet: none
Armour: probably very little
Opponents: other Gregarii, fighting in
  groups or in mock battles

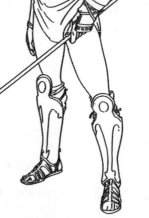

A selected list of Scribo titles

The prices shown below are correct at the time of going to press. However, The Salariya Book Company reserves the right to show new retail prices on covers, which may differ from those previously advertised.

Gladiator School by Dan Scott

1 Blood Oath	978-1-908177-48-3	£6.99
2 Blood & Fire	978-1-908973-60-3	£6.99
3 Blood & Sand	978-1-909645-16-5	£6.99
4 Blood Vengeance	978-1-909645-62-2	£6.99
5 Blood & Thunder	978-1-910184-20-2	£6.99
6 Blood Justice *(Spring 2015)*	978-1-910184-43-1	£6.99

Iron Sky by Alex Woolf

1 Dread Eagle	978-1-909645-00-4	£6.99

Aldo Moon by Alex Woolf

1 Aldo Moon and the Ghost at Gravewood Hall		
	978-1-908177-84-1	£6.99

Chronosphere by Alex Woolf

1 Time out of Time	978-1-907184-55-0	£6.99
2 Malfunction	978-1-907184-56-7	£6.99
3 Ex Tempora	978-1-908177-87-2	£6.99

Visit our website at:

www.salariya.com

All Scribo and Salariya Book Company titles can be ordered from your local bookshop, or by post from:

The Salariya Book Co. Ltd,
25 Marlborough Place
Brighton BN1 1UB

Postage and packing **free** in the United Kingdom

GLADIATOR SCHOOL
BOOK 5

BLOOD & THUNDER

GLADIATOR SCHOOL
BOOK 5

BLOOD & THUNDER

POSTULATUS
'the Favourite'

Weapons: **mace or flail, and sword**
Shield: **none**
Helmet: **full-face with grille-covered eye holes**
Armour: **manica (arm guard), greaves (shin guards)**
Opponents: **Noxii (criminals), in special display fights before the emperor**

GREGARIUS
'the Common Gladiator'

Weapon: **probably spear or sword**
Shield: **none**
Helmet: **none**
Armour: **probably very little**
Opponents: **other Gregarii, fighting in groups or in mock battles**

www.scribobooks.com/gladiatorschool
© MMXV The Salariya Book Company Ltd

www.scribobooks.com/gladiatorschool
© MMXV The Salariya Book Company Ltd

GLADIATOR SCHOOL
BOOK 5

BLOOD & THUNDER

CALEDONIAN WARRIOR

Weapons: **long sword and spear**
Shield: **long, oval**
Helmet: **metal and leather**
Armour: **none**
Opponents: **the Romans and, sometimes, other British tribes**

GLADIATOR SCHOOL
BOOK 5

BLOOD & THUNDER

ROMAN LEGIONARY

Weapons: **spear (pilum), short sword (gladius), dagger (pugio)**
Shield: **large, rectangular, curved**
Helmet: **domed, with neck and cheek protectors**
Armour: **cuirass (breastplate) of metal hoops over leather**
Opponents: **anyone who threatens the borders of the Roman empire**